Paul T. Mascia is a *cum laude* graduate of Yale University, where he majored in Religious Studies. His senior thesis was an in-depth analysis of the reformer and Medieval mystic, St Catherine of Siena. Paul has attained over thirty years of experience as an insurance professional with an expertise in the fields of both long-term care and disability insurance. He has a certification in long term care planning (CLTC). Paul and his wife, Theresa, currently live in Columbus, OH. They have five adult children and seven grandchildren. *Nazar's Journey* is Mr. Mascia's first novel, and his first piece of historical fiction. His work aims to realise two important goals during this season of his life: a desire to utilise his creative skills in new ways, as well as to draw attention to the sufferings of displaced peoples in diverse parts of the globe, particularly those facing severe adversity due to their religious beliefs.

This book is dedicated to my father, Anthony R. Mascia, MD, who supervised a medical clinic for the Allies in Cherbourg, France, soon after the D Day invasion in the summer of 1944—as well as two other infirmaries in Deauville, France and Brussels, Belgium. My father taught me about the inestimable value of each human life. He frequently lamented that wars not only cause immense tragedy and human suffering, but they impoverish our world of countless talents and gifts due to the loss of many millions of lives, cut short in the prime of youth.

I also dedicate this book to a beloved theologian, whose many reflections on how beauty opens the soul to God inspired me to create this work.

To those of us who live in comfort, security, and peace, may this story be a reminder of the millions of innocent civilians of the twentieth century and our current century, who, through no fault of their own, were brutally forced to leave behind their homes and livelihoods forever, journeying towards a future of profound hardship, uncertainty, and poverty.

Paul T. Mascia

Nazar's Journey

Austin Macauley Publishers

Copyright © Paul T. Mascia 2024

The right of Paul T. Mascia to be identified as author of this work has been asserted by the author in accordance with sections 77 and 78 of the Copyright, Designs and Patents Act 1988.

All rights reserved. No part of this publication may be reproduced, stored in a retrieval system, or transmitted in any form or by any means, electronic, mechanical, photocopying, recording, or otherwise, without the prior permission of the publishers.

Any person who commits any unauthorised act in relation to this publication may be liable to criminal prosecution and civil claims for damages.

This is a work of fiction. Names, characters, businesses, places, events, locales, and incidents are either the products of the author's imagination or used in a fictitious manner. Any resemblance to actual persons, living or dead, or actual events is purely coincidental.

A CIP catalogue record for this title is available from the British Library.

ISBN 9781035822720 (Paperback)
ISBN 9781035822737 (ePub e-book)

www.austinmacauley.com

First Published 2024
Austin Macauley Publishers Ltd®
1 Canada Square
Canary Wharf
London
E14 5AA

The creation of *Nazar's Journey* was significantly influenced, spurred on, and shaped by many friends over a three-year period. For all of you, I am profoundly grateful, not only for your help, but for *who you are*.

My beloved wife, Theresa, and all of our family members, in particular Maria Mascia and Catherine Williamson, were my secret spring of love and support, motivating me to keep calm and carry on to the finish line.

Perry Cahall, PhD, the academic dean at the Josephinum, as well as a friend and mentor, was one of the first non-family members to review the draft of my manuscript, encouraging me to pursue publication.

Joop Koopman, the Communications Director for the Aid to the Church in Need in Brooklyn, NY, has been a constant and reliable source of practical help and advice from the very beginning of the project to its completion.

Stephen M. Rasche, author of *The Disappearing People*, generously shared his first-hand knowledge of Karemlesh, the Nineveh plains, and the culture of Iraq with me, allowing me to authenticate many historical details. On more than one occasion, he reviewed my manuscript to make sure the plot elements were consistent with the events of 2014.

Joseph Head, a friend of many years, offered me many hours of editorial and creative help as the manuscript expanded and evolved.

John Cerullo, a true gentleman with a lifetime of publishing experience, affirmed early on that my story should be in print. John patiently guided me through the process of finding a reputable publisher that would be the right fit for *Nazar's Journey*.

Dr. Richard Fitzgerald, Amanda Mole, and the choir of St Joseph Cathedral here in Columbus inspired me to create the scene under the stars. I was attending Compline in the solemn candle-lit cathedral one evening when I heard Richard's composition of the Psalm 90 (91) antiphon sung by the choir—"He will conceal you in His wings. You will not fear the terror of the night." While listening to this transporting piece, the scene of Amira and Nazar gazing up at the stars suddenly appeared in my imagination.

Mother Olga Yacob of the Daughters of Mary of Nazareth, Deacon Sermed Ashkouri, Qais Al Sindy, and Fady Aqrawi are Americans who grew up in Iraq and know the language and culture intimately. They were pivotal in providing the expressions in Sureth, a form of Aramaic used in Nineveh, which I included in my dialogues. The translation of the words from Psalm 91 into Sureth was done by Fady.

Brother Joe Donovan, a graduate of the Pennsylvania Academy of Fine Arts, a friend and longtime member of the Brotherhood of Hope, was my artistic advisor regarding the cover design. He created the imaginative Tolkienesque map which is found at the start of this book.

Although I could devote a page to each of these individuals who took their time to read my manuscript and write such fine endorsements, for brevity sake I will simply mention their names as an expression of my deep appreciation for their efforts: Weam Namou, Gabriel Meyer, Dr. Aaron Urbanczyk, Ismail Royer, and Father Ben Kiely. I am also profoundly grateful for Joseph Pearce's encouragement and his inspiring introduction, and for Stephen Rasche's insightful Afterword. The amazing paintings of Qais Al Sindy are described in detail in my About the Artwork. I cannot express in words how much I appreciate his collaboration. His boundless creativity exceeded all my expectations.

I am also grateful to the following individuals, who offered me assistance by reviewing or critiquing my work, by words of encouragement, or by their prayers:

Sister Mary Ann Fatula, PhD, Rachel and Chris Padian, Fr. Timothy Lynch, Carol, Sarah, and Hannah Stollenwerk, John Hack, Brendan O'Rourke, Fr. Matthew Morris, Joseph M. Mascia, Matt Palmer, M. Lennon Perricone, John Donelan, Nathaniel Earls, Dr. Bruce Fraser, Michael O'Brien, Debra Esolen, Jim Haban, Carlos Posada, Amira and Erdal Unver, Fr. Peter John Cameron, Fr. Bernard Marie of the Franciscan Friars in London, Dr. Linus Meldrum, Brother Jude LaSota,

Gregory C. Floyd, Tom Morris, Paul Wills, Dr Marlon De La Torre, Mark Huddy, George Rushman, Dick Hintershied, Michael Agriesti, Jerry Freewalt, Albert Vautour, Chris Schweitzer, Irene and Bill Brundage and Peter Krajnak.

Finally, I am indebted to several writer-saints whom I have frequently implored for inspiration—St Paul, Therese of Lisieux, Teresa of Avila, John Henry Newman, Thomas Aquinas, and, of course, Catherine of Siena.

Endorsements

Nazar's Journey is a moving and thought-provoking work of historical fiction that depicts the real events of the Nineveh Plains of Iraq in August of 2014. The novel skilfully weaves together themes of war, persecution, redemption, and faith, inviting readers to imagine themselves in the situation of the characters, unable to return to their homes. The story follows Nazar, a young Christian boy who is forced into adulthood by the crisis that befalls his village. As he makes his way to safety with others, we're taken on a journey that is both harrowing and inspiring. Along the way, Nazar encounters both profound evil and the consistent presence and protection of God's love and providence.

Author Paul Mascia's writing is both poetic and spiritual, creating a vivid and immersive reading experience. The characters are well-drawn and relatable, and their journeys will stay with readers long after they have finished the book.

As a native Christian Iraqi, *Nazar's Journey* sparked many emotions and memories of my ancestral land in northern Iraq. My favourite passage was this: We have lived through so much sorrow in our land now, so many thousands who have lost fathers or mothers or brothers or sisters. So many badly hurt or wounded. So many homes and shops abandoned—so much destruction—everywhere. Let us not lose hope, even if we don't understand where the good Lord is leading us, or what the future may bring.

Weam Namou is the Executive Director of the Chaldean Cultural Centre in Michigan, an Eric Hoffer award-winning author of 16 books, and multi-award-winning filmmaker of two feature films.

****

As a devout Muslim and a scholar of Islam, I loved reading *Nazar's Journey*. It is an extraordinary piece of historical fiction, very well written, with many compelling moral and spiritual themes. I was inspired by the Muslim characters in this evocative story. The device of the Skylark was particularly beautiful. In our violent and tumultuous world, the author presents his hopeful vision for a future of cooperation and charity among peaceful Muslims and sincere Christians.

Ismail Royer, Director of Islam and Religious Freedom, Religious Freedom Institute, Washington, DC.

****

Nazar's Journey is a beautiful gem of a story. In the midst of terror, war, and oppression among modern-day Christians in the Middle East, *Nazar's Journey* tells a tale of persistent faith, hope, and redemption.

Dr. Aaron Urbanczyk, Professor of English, Franciscan University, Steubenville.

****

This delightful book, a tale of love and hope in a time of terror, brings the terrible suffering of Iraqi Christians, so ignored by most in the West, to our attention. Having visited Nineveh, the ancient home of Iraqi Christians since the time of the Apostles, I know that this lovely story has an authenticity and simplicity which reflect the deep truths it tells. A story, like this one, allows the statistics about persecuted Christians to be given a name and a face.

Father Benedict Kiely, Founder of Nasarean, org, which helps persecuted Christians globally.

****

A lack of appreciation for the witness of the ancient Churches of the Middle East is one of the blind spots of the Christian West. Many modern Christians are virtually unaware that vibrant Christian communities, though perennially threatened, still exist in Syria, Iraq, and Iran, and elsewhere in the region, rooted in traditions that hearken back to apostolic times.

Paul T. Mascia's lyrical saga, *Nazar's Journey*, takes us into that world—a world ripped from today's headlines, characterised by crisis, instability, war, flight, and exile. And by faith, humanity, resourcefulness, loyalty, and hope. As a former war correspondent, I can attest to the realism and skill with which Mascia paints the dizzying disorientations of violent conflict, the sudden rending of the fabric of families, the chaos of refugees frantic to survive.

But the "journey" of the title is not merely a chronicle of war and survival—it is a chronicle of a spiritual journey as well, a "coming of age" novel about a youth who discovers inner resources in the midst of war, and the insights which only faith can provide.

Nazar's Journey—a tale with all the simplicity of a Medieval legend and all the timeliness of this morning's newscast.

Gabriel Meyer is an award-winning foreign war correspondent and the author of *In the Shade of the Terebinth: Tales of a Night Journey*.

Nazar, a boy of almost 14, has enjoyed a peaceful and idyllic life on a simple farm in the Nineveh Plains of Iraq, where he routinely helped his father with the chores, attended the small village school in Karemlesh, and played soccer with his friends when he had free time. But then, radical militants conquer the city of Mosul and suddenly sweep through the entire region of the Nineveh Plains in a tsunami of terror, and Nazar's quiet world is abruptly torn apart. He is suddenly forced to make challenging decisions when he observes, with horror, his own people frantically running away from the quiet village he grew up in, trying desperately to escape to safety. Within hours, he will leave his boyhood behind forever and will undertake a journey which will shape him into a young man of extraordinary selflessness and courage.

Nazar's Journey
Introduction
By Joseph Pearce

The story you are about to read is hopeful in the fullest and most literal sense of the word. It is full of hope. And yet, paradoxically, it is set in the midst of one of the grimmest and deadliest episodes in recent history in which it would have been very easy for people to lose all hope.

    The story takes place on the plains of Nineveh in Iraq. It is August 2014. Islamic State militants have captured the Christian town of Qaraqosh. The Kurdish troops who were the Christians' only defence have retreated. Those Christians who are not killed, flee in terror from their homes, headed for the town of Erbil, forty miles to the east in Kurdistan. Most are on foot. It is the hottest time of the year. Many are old or sick. There are many infants and children. Food and water are scarce. Many die by the side of the road and are buried in the shallowest of graves by their grieving family members. There are no tools for the digging of adequate graves. There is no time. Within days, the bodies are decaying. The stench of death fills the hot, stifling air as the tens of thousands of refugees trudge eastwards towards relative safety. Perhaps, in such extreme and horrific conditions, it would be understandable were people to lose hope.

Nazar, the thirteen-year-old eponymous hero of this story, is on a journey which is much more than a flight to safety. His journey is a quest to find his father. It is a journey in faith, animated by love, but it is full of hope.

Hope, as the humblest of virtues, is the antidote to the poison of pride, the greatest of sins. Hope overthrows pride with humility. Where hope prevails, pride fails. Conversely, where hope is absent, pride prevails. Hopelessness is despair, and despair is the triumph of pride. Hope, the humble David of the virtues, slays the mighty Goliath of the sins.

Hope also has a special place in ancient mythology, a place reserved for it in Pandora's Box, which, ironically, was not really Pandora's at all. It belonged to the gods and she had no right to open it. As with Eve's plucking of the forbidden fruit, Pandora, the pagan Eve, opens the forbidden box. The curse of this original sin plagues humanity as, like a cloud of licentious locusts, vice and disease pour forth from the opened casket, along with wars, terrorism and hatred of Christ and His Church. Only hope remains in the box, the silver lining in the cloud that overshadows fallen humanity.

Hope is also the silver lining in the cloud that overshadows Nazar and the other characters whom he meets. It is ever present, like the God whom Nazar trusts. At times, Nazar is a figure of the true disciple who takes up his cross on his very own via dolorosa in imitation of Christ. His separation from his beloved father reflects the agony of the Son's separation from the Father in the Garden of Gethsemane. Even his name is an abbreviated form of "Nazarene". Perhaps we might even see Nazar as a Christ figure in the sense that he is joined on the journey by an old man called Yousif, i.e. Joseph, and a woman called Amira, the grouping of an old man, younger woman and a child serving as an emblematic representation of the Holy Family on the flight to Egypt. This is surely intentional on the author's part considering that Amira first introduces Yousif to Nazar in words which connect him to St Joseph: "He is a builder. Just like St Joseph. That's his name, you know—Yousif."

It says something for the poetic quality of Paul T. Mascia's storytelling that the presence of hope is signified metaphorically at key moments in the story by the appearance of the Skylark, which ascends in song in the very midst of the evil and descends dovelike as the suggestive presence of the Holy Spirit. The song of the Skylark raises the curtain epigraphically on the story, or rather, and to be precise, it is Shelley's song "To a Skylark" which raises the curtain and sets the scene. In this wonderful poem, one of the most beautiful ever written, we hear the poet's own worded song of praise to the Skylark's wordless song. Although seeming to have little to do with the ugliness of the situation in which Nazar finds himself, the recurrence of the metaphorical presence of the Skylark as a musical motif signifies a bird's-eye view of the events unfolding on the ground, suggestive of the presence of a beauty which transcends the ugliness of sin, death and war, and which transfigures the darkest moments with the light and love of God's presence. At one such moment, Nazar asks Amira the deepest of questions, receiving in response the wisest of replies:

Amira went out with Nazar into the wheat fields. There was a soothing summer evening breeze passing through the fields and stirring the harvest. The crickets and other night creatures were making pleasant melodies. They looked up at the sky. Amira was stunned by the glittering lights. Nazar almost felt like he could reach up and touch them and bring them to earth. When they began to talk, the Skylark woke up from his deep sleep and listened to their conversation.

"Amira?"

"Yes, Nazar."

"You talk about the good Lord. Le bon Dieu."

"Yes, that's right."

"But, Amira, do you really believe that God is good? Now that we see all the terrible things that have happened to us…"

Amira's eyes remained fixed on the heavens.

"Nazar, would a Tashya Alousa create such beauty?"

Amira was using the Chaldean words for cruel tyrant.

Nazar paused. He could not answer.

Then Amira put her arm on his shoulder. "Yes, Nazar, the suffering is real. But the goodness is inescapable. It is surrounding us."

Apart from the beauty of creation, resplendent in the night sky and in the song of the Skylark, there is also the deep beauty to be found in the dignity of the human person and the holiness of souls. Nazar sees such beauty when he first meets Amira. He recognises "a beauty in her countenance, a beauty which any artist would be challenged to depict". Nor is such beauty something merely physical: "It was an inner beauty, perhaps emanating from the depths of her soul, a beauty which endures and even flourishes with the passage of time."

There is one other connection to the Skylark, presumably unintended by the author, which warrants our attention. A few years ago, back in 2007 to be precise, a novel was published by Antonia Arslan, entitled *Skylark Farm*, which is very similar in terms of genre and subject matter to *Nazar's Journey*. This earlier novel is set amidst the Armenian Genocide of the early twentieth century, a hundred years before the "ethnic cleansing" of the Christians of Iraq by Islamist extremists. *Skylark Farm*, along with Arslan's follow-up novel, *Silent Angel*, dovetail very well with *Nazar's Journey* as works of historical fiction which highlight the anti-Christian pogroms of modern times.

We will end this brief introduction to this brief but powerful story with a discussion of how the story ends. We will do so, however, without giving away the plot or without any "spoilers".

The story ends with a *eucatastrophe*, a word invented by J. R. R. Tolkien to indicate the sudden joyous turn in a story which leads to the consolation of the happy ending. *Eucatastrophe* is the antithesis of *catastrophe*, which is the sudden devastating turn which leads to tragedy. It offers what Tolkien called the "sudden glimpse of the underlying reality or truth ... a brief vision...a far-off gleam or echo of *evangelium*". *Evangelium*. Good news!

Without saying exactly what happens, which is for the reader to discover, we can reveal that *Nazar's Journey* ends with a sudden joyous turn and the consolation of a happy ending. How can a story filled with the suggestive presence of the Fatherhood of God end in any other way?

Joseph Pearce is a literary critic, a historian, and a Shakespeare scholar. He is the author of thirty books, including *Tolkien: Man and Myth* and *Solzhenitsyn: A Soul in Exile*.

About the Artwork

As I was writing *Nazar's Journey*, I had hoped to locate an artist from Iraq who could do some black pen sketches for the novella. My concept was to provide the reader with a direct link to the heritage and culture of Iraq, and I thought that perhaps an artist of Iraqi background could accomplish this personal connection. Initially I was looking for an art student, someone at the start of her career, who would benefit from working on this project.

Instead, providentially, something entirely different happened. I was able to meet Qais Al Sindy, an accomplished and highly skilled artist, whose work has been exhibited all over the world. Qais was initially a competent engineering student at the University of Baghdad. After graduation his objectives changed, and he went on to attain an MFA at the Academy of Fine Arts in 2004. From a political perspective, he refused to join the Baath party, and that same year, at the age of 37, he left his homeland. Recall that the American military intervention in Iraq began in 2003, so his personal exodus took place during the war. Qais now resides in California. Our new friendship not only gifted this project with a highly talented artist, but a person who grew up in Iraq and knows the culture intimately.

When Qais read my manuscript, he identified with—and immediately embraced—my goal of making better known, through means of a story, the extraordinary suffering of thousands of innocent people in modern Iraq, who faced the innumerable tragedies that war sets in motion, who were persecuted for their faith and then forced to abruptly leave their villages and their homeland. He was also keenly aware of the implications of the Nineveh microcosm for other cultures and periods of history, as we hear about millions of people who are currently exiled from their homelands. The suffering of the innocent continues in our day.

In addition to his three Skylark sketches, Qais was inspired to create for Nazar's Journey nine oil paintings which are masterpieces. Rather than illustrate the various scenes of my story, he was compelled to go a different route. His paintings convey universal themes which he felt were inspired by the characters of the novella. The profound messages embedded in his paintings include displacement—the shock of leaving one's homeland, the human cost of war, grieving the violent loss of a loved one, the process of maturation from boyhood to manhood, the yearning for freedom, the enduring power of hope, and the bond between love and self-sacrifice. By means of his painting, he wishes to bring comfort and healing to his own people, as well as offer solace to many other diverse peoples throughout the globe who have experienced similar trials. Like my story, he has portrayed suffering, but he has also portrayed the beauty of hope. To quote Mr. Al Sindy: "These paintings are a testament to the resilience of the human spirit in the face of adversity. I believe that art, much like storytelling, allows individuals to empathise with the experiences of others and encourages introspection."

As I have spoken with the artist about his vision for each of his expressionist works, I am providing for the reader a brief note on each of them here. Even though I am disclosing what he has conveyed to me, he would like the viewer to also use his own imagination and reach her own conclusions about the meaning of the paintings. One thing is certain: the works are compelling. They stop you in your tracks. They pull you away from the predictable routine of daily life and make you ask the question, "What would life be like for me, attempting to survive in that situation? Would I have the strength to endure such adversity and continue moving forward?"

Spoiler Alert:

The paintings are placed in the book so that they will not give the reader any plot clues ahead of time. I suggest that, rather than reading the following notes prior to reading the novella, that you read the specific painting details as you come across the image in the normal flow of the story.

Painting #1
The Greater Love

If you look carefully at this work, you will notice a father figure, assisted by his wife, who appear to be carrying a very heavy burden, perhaps someone sick or elderly, along with their two children. The title of the work references the words of Jesus, who said there is no greater love than to lay down one's lives for one's friend. (John 15:13) The love of parents for their children can indeed be a self-sacrificial love. Such love is carried to the limits in situations of war, persecution, and displacement. The box that they are standing on symbolises the homeland.

Painting #2
Pieta of Mosul

This evocative work is a pieta, not depicting Mary mourning over the body of her crucified Son, but instead showing Nazar grieving over the violent act which was inflicted on his mother, Mary. This image relates to the scene in Mar Addai where Nazar kneels on the church floor and weeps over the vandalised statue, which conveys deep memories of his own beloved mother.

Here, the artist brilliantly positions Nazar holding the head of the statue of the Virgin in his hands. Note that the head is not from Karemlesh, but from Rome, a duplicate of Michelangelo's masterpiece. Since Mosul is the principal city of the Nineveh province, the artist has named his work Pieta of Mosul.

Nazar is depicted as taller than his age, just as the Mary figure in Michelangelo's pieta is disproportionately large. Perhaps his suffering is sculpting him into mature manhood. Nazar's open hand of the Mosul pieta mimics the open hand of Mary in the Roman pieta. It symbolises total acceptance of the will of God, even in adversity.

Painting #3
Of Old Sat Freedom on the Heights

This work depicts the Holy Family—Joseph, Jesus and Mary—in flight from Bethlehem to Egypt, as has been represented by countless artists over the centuries. The figures are flying in the air. Flight for the artist symbolises freedom.

The box at the bottom of the composition represents the homeland, which must be abruptly abandoned.

The name of the artwork is identical to the title of Alfred, Lord Tennyson's poem personifying freedom as a woman. The poem highlights the theme of political freedom from injustice and oppression. The artist likewise expresses the quest for both political and spiritual freedom in this painting, which portrays the Holy Family escaping in haste from the violence and madness of King Herod.

Painting #4
An Attempt to Fly

This work depicts the figure of Nazar, vigorous and robust, pushing himself off the ground as if he were a bird ready to take off in flight. The Skylark is directly above him, the symbol of his transcendent source of strength and inspiration, motivating him to seek freedom from all that has wounded and crippled him. Once again, for Mr. Al Sindy, flight symbolises freedom.

Painting #5
So That We May Return Home

This is perhaps the most perplexing of the artworks. We see Nazar facing east towards Erbil, hopefully a destination of safety and freedom.

We also see directly behind him a spectre, symbolising his father, whom he loves deeply. Nazar is worried about Baba, whether he is still alive, or whether he was killed by the militants.

Nazar is attached to a burden of memories of beloved family and friends, beautiful and terrible memories, represented by the figure of the upside-down face of a boy or man. He is carrying the heavy weight of suffering—seen in dark swirls of brushwork. His emotions of love, fear, and grief are all trying to pull him down and cripple him.

Yet he is determined to move forward. He has resolved to go east to Erbil, to freedom, even while carrying this unbearable weight of memory, a weight which cannot completely be left behind.

Perhaps he will return to his village in Nineveh and his homeland, symbolised by the roots at the bottom of the painting.

Perhaps he will find a new home somewhere else on the planet where he will discover love and healing.

Painting #6
He Will Conceal You in His Wings

This stunningly luminous painting was done by the artist at my request. It depicts the scene under the stars in the story, with Nazar and Amira standing in the wheat fields while gazing at the heavens. The artist has changed one significant detail. In my story, Amira puts her arm on Nazar's shoulder to comfort the young man. In contrast, in this painting, a taller and more mature Nazar is gently embracing Amira's shoulder. The white light shining on Nazar's arm seems to suggest a bird with outstretched wings. The visual narrative thus portrays Nazar as the image of God who, to quote the artist, "bears the suffering for the salvation of His faithful people, symbolised here by Amira."

Qais has also introduced the symbol of the key: "Nazar's left hand holds a key, a powerful symbol of his hopeful belief of returning home. This is affirmed by the appearance of a comet in the night sky as Amira chants the verse from Psalm 91:

He will conceal you in His wings.

You will not fear the terror of the night."

Mr. Al Sindy surprised me by painting these very words in Sureth, the language spoken in Nineveh, at the bottom of the composition.

He also conveyed to me that he sees the stars as emblematic of the saints, who are looking down from heaven, encouraging and interceding for us in the midst of our earthly pilgrimage.

Painting #7
The Sacrifice of the War

The biblical figure of Abraham from Ur of the Chaldees in Mesopotamia, present day Iraq, is a spiritual father figure for three global faiths: Judaism, Christianity, and Islam.

Here, the Abraham figure is holding his son who has been killed or is severely wounded. In the Biblical story, Abraham is held back from sacrificing his son Isaac by the intervention of an angel. But in this depiction, no such intervention takes place. Decisions were made at the highest levels of government which ultimately required the sacrifice of this young man's life. Is there a purpose or meaning in the sacrifice? That is the question the painting compels us to ask.

Painting #8
The Woman Who Carried Her Country Over Her Head

The woman appears to be apprehensive and disoriented. She is not only carrying her meagre physical belongings with her. She is carrying her memories, both the beautiful and the traumatic. She must continue her exodus. She must get up and move on, but the future is uncertain. Directly behind her you will see the shadow of an ox, an ancient Mesopotamian symbol of perseverance, determination, resilience, and strength.

Painting #9
Maternity Passion

The artist has suggested a scene from the Nazar story where the Virgin Mary returns to visit the young man to comfort him in his trauma and distress. She is no longer a statue. Rather, she has come alive, like a warm and caring mother. She embraces Nazar in his moment of agony.

"I will lead the blind
by a road they do not know.
By paths they have not known
I will guide them.
I will turn the darkness before them into light,
The rough places into level ground." Isaiah 42:16

The Skylark

Hail to thee, blithe Spirit!
Higher still and higher
From the earth thou springest
The blue deep thou wingest,
And singing still dost soar,
And soaring ever singest.

Percy Bysshe Shelley—*To a Skylark*

There are many unique birds in the Nineveh Plains of Iraq which sing beautiful melodies, and one of these is the Skylark.

It was a bright, clear mid-August morning outside the village of Karemlesh. Perched high on a branch of a tall eucalyptus tree surrounded by golden wheat fields, the Skylark began to sing, his brown feathers dappled with white proudly glistening in the daylight. Once he was greeted by the rising sun, he usually shook his wings to stretch them out after his night's sleep, then he would soar high into the deep blue sky and travel into the old town. No bird in Iraq could soar like the Skylark. He perched on the roof of Mar Addai, the ancient church dedicated to St Thaddeus, and surveyed his surroundings.

Only a few days ago, when day-to-day life was completely normal, everyone from the village recognised and savoured the joyful flute-like sounds which trilled from his beak each morning. His heavenly music flowed through the streets like the pleasant ripples of a spring stream.

The villagers counted on his morning song to wash away all the fears, as well as the loneliness and silence of night.

But now his melody was suddenly changed—troubled, muted, confused. His song was no longer a rushing fountain, but instead a trickle, like the sound of dripping water.

Something is wrong, thought the Skylark as he watched over the village.

I have summoned the villagers to awake. I have called out—rejoice! The darkness of night is no more, and the bright morning sun now gazes over the land.

The wheat fields are awaiting the harvest. Awake!

The Skylark's sharp eyes gazed down on the town from his vantage point next to the cross, atop the pinnacle of Mar Addai. Not a single man or woman could be found scurrying along the village streets on their way to the fields. There were no farmers wheeling their carts to set up their fruit and vegetable stands at the marketplace near the church. There were no elderly people sweeping their steps or going out for their daily walk.

Then the Skylark spotted Nazar, one of the older boys of the village—lying asleep against a crumbled wall.

The Skylark knew Nazar and his family, *Well, Nazar,* grumbled the Skylark to himself, *you should be at home now doing your morning farm chores with your father and your brother Samir. What are you doing here in the village? Are you sick? Why are you resting against that wall?*

The Skylark stared impatiently at the young man who truthfully could no longer be called a boy. He was growing up quickly, yet he had so much more to learn about life. His legs had gotten much longer over the years. He had learned to run fast. His face was becoming handsome, perhaps even noble, though at that moment it was smeared with dirt and sweat. But he would not stir.

The Skylark was puzzled. He remembered the sounds of thunder that he heard during the night, sounds that were invading the quiet of his sleep. *Perhaps the sounds were not coming from thunder after all*, he thought, *but from those human war machines that seemed to be constantly cursing the beauty and serenity of his homeland.* He had heard the dreaded sounds of those war machines crossing his territory, too many times during his lifetime.

He kept wondering why Nazar was sleeping outside on the ground, damp with the morning dew, instead of inside his comfortable old stone farmhouse. Could the troubling sounds of the night have anything to do with Nazar's situation? He flew down from the roof of Mar Addai to a little bush nearby, peeking closely at Nazar's face. Nazar seemed to be breathing slowly. His cheek was bruised. His face appeared agitated, even in sleep. He was moaning quietly, but the Skylark did not understand his words.

Then he observed that Nazar's arm was stretched out in the road—bleeding. The Skylark suddenly became very troubled, so he raised his crest abruptly as if to sound an alarm. He squawked for help—but no one answered.

Then he soared high into the blue morning Nineveh sky and disappeared.

Nightmare of Cruel Memories

Nazar had been dreaming so he didn't hear the Skylark.

His dreams were vivid and frightening, causing his whole body to shiver.

In his dreams, he could hear the explosions from mortar rounds and rocket propelled grenades.

He could hear the cries and piercing lamentations of women and children who were leaving their homes and all their belongings behind, as they fled the village in the night.

He could see bullets swirling around him—swarms of bullets like the cruel hailstorms which pricked his skin and fiercely battered his farmhouse in the dead of winter.

In the darkness of his dream, he could not see where the bullets were coming from, who was firing the bullets, neither who nor what they were shooting at.

He could see windows being shattered and dark smoke engulfing him. He could smell the putrid odour of burning rubber filling the air. He saw cars and trucks destroyed and toppled over in flames.

Then he saw a dozen enemy tanks far in the distance, along the horizon, moving out from the city of Mosul en route to the other villages of the Nineveh plains. It was sunset and the golden rays of the sun reflected off the shiny metal of the enormous tanks. It was anything but a beautiful scene. It was frightening.

Still trapped in the fog of his dream, he saw himself running into Karemlesh as it was getting dark. Villagers of all ages, many of whom he had known all the years of his life—were streaming out of the gates of the village, passing him by as he went the opposite way, pushing against each other; fathers shouting, babies crying, mothers doing their best to carry out a few valuables and mementos in bundles while attempting to huddle their children together—filled with only a small portion of their belongings.

As the dream continued, he was suddenly transported to the small grocery and butcher shop next to the church, owned by his father's close friend, Aram. Although it was after store hours and the shop was dark, Nazar noticed that the entrance door was still open, and he walked inside. Most of the ceiling and counter lights were turned off. There were no customers in the store. Aram was bending over the counter, weeping. The dim streetlight streaming through the shop window created a portrait of utter desolation.

Nazar had decided to go there first after entering the village that evening. He was determined to ask Aram if he knew where his father had gone.

Aram recognised the voice of the young man. He did not look up at Nazar because he was in such a state of grief. He pounded his fist on the counter, crying out, "All of my work, all of this food and these groceries in this shop that I have paid for…I have been here for 14 years, I have had a successful business in Karemlesh since before you were born, and now they are telling me that I must leave it all behind." He looked up at last and revealed his distraught face to Nazar. Then he frantically paced around his shop, pointing to the various meats. "Do you know how painful this is for me and my family, Nazar? This is a disaster. All this meat will be rotten when I return. Look at this beautiful baby lamb. Look at these sausages and chicken and chops. This lamb just arrived today. We are likely to lose power—I am certain of that, and when I return, this place will have the stench of death. If not, those wolves—who call themselves warriors, when they break in here, they will steal everything—every last egg, every sausage, every crust of bread. Nazar, I don't know what I am going to do."

Aram's face was drenched with tears and his eyes blazed red with fear and rage.

Nazar hesitantly put his hand on Aram's shoulder, "Aram, I don't know what to say. I am so sorry." Then he stood by for several minutes of silence as Aram continued to weep and utter sounds which came from the depths of his soul. He had never seen Aram this way. Aram—a cheerful, jovial, caring man whom everyone in Karemlesh loved, he could not hide his inner turmoil from Nazar. Then, when Aram stopped crying, he wiped his tear-soaked face with his soiled apron, Nazar said, "Aram, let me help you for a while. I see there is that big mutton hanging outside under the awning, and flies are landing on it. Why don't I help you bring it inside? We can put it in the refrigerator, or maybe the freezer if there is room."

Then, at last, he asked Aram if he knew where his father was, explaining that he had not seen him at all that day.

Without telling him about any of the other horrifying events he had just witnessed with his own eyes at his Uncle Basim's farm, in a daze Nazar mumbled, "I saw terrible things out in the fields, Aram…I was so frightened I sped like the wind. I got here as quickly as I could. I did not want to go back to our farmhouse and stay there alone. I used a beat-up motorbike from my Uncle Basim—I wish it rode faster, but it worked for me…and, Aram," he gulped in fear, "along the road not too far from here, I just saw some cars and trucks overturned and burning. My motorbike ran out of gas close to the town, and I ran the rest of the way. It was the fastest I have ever run in my life."

Aram, forgetting himself for a moment, looked at the young man, "I have never seen your face like this, Nazar. Your face is filled with terror. Look at you, you are trembling. I think perhaps…your sufferings may even be greater than mine." He gave Nazar a hug.

There was a moment of complete silence. Nazar felt comforted by Aram, but he could not cry.

"I am so very sorry, Nazar, as I do not know where your father went today," he paused a moment, thinking, "but I can tell you that your father was helping some elderly people in the old part of the town, pack up some of their belongings, and then I did see him carrying them into cars and trucks to get them to evacuate, but that was early this morning maybe over ten hours ago."

"Evacuate?"

"Do not ask me to explain now, we are all being told to get out of Karemlesh, the sooner the better. Nazar, don't worry about my shop. I will finish up here. You must go around town right away and look for your father. He may still be here, maybe with the elderly. I will lock up the shop and then go join my family who are packing up whatever they can take. It won't be much, that I know…maybe you should just stay with us? What do you think? We could catch up with your father later."

Nazar knew what he had to do, "No, Aram, it is still early, I will go around town and keep looking."

The dream then allowed Nazar to see himself almost as in a blurred mirror. He was anxiously running through the streets of the village as darkness smothered the town. The streets were dimly lit and never seemed to end as he zig-zagged through the labyrinth of the old town, then into the newer part of the village. Everywhere Karemlesh was immersed in chaos and panic. He called out while endless clusters of villagers passed him by, 'Baba! Baba! Baba!' He looked to the right and to the left to see if his father was there in the dense crowds. He ran down the alleyways, went into the abandoned shops, knocked on the doors of all the houses that he knew, but there was no answer to his cries for help.

He cried out—'Baba! Baba! Baba!'

But his father was gone.

As the evening turned to night, outside of the village Nazar thought he heard the roaring of thunder in the distance. But it was not thunder. There were more repeated explosions from the rocket propelled grenades and mortars. In his dream, these horrid sounds got louder and louder, causing his head to pound. Then there were rapidly flashing images of glass shattering, concrete and debris from buildings cascading near him. The streets of the town were cluttered with abandoned cars and carts. More bullets were swirling around him, bullets spewing from the guns of evil fighters he could not see. And, in the darkness, he could not tell who or what the enemy was aiming at.

Then, in this prolonged and tortuous nightmare, he was brought back in time to the shocking event that happened just before he sprinted into the village that evening and saw Aram at his shop.

Some dreams have a way of confusing time and sequence, exaggerating the bad memories and minimising the good ones. But there was no exaggeration of the evil in this last sequence of his dream. In a strange way, his troubled mind had saved the cruellest memory for last.

Nazar's body trembled even while he slept on in semi-consciousness. Nazar had hitched a ride to get closer to his Uncle Basim's property, which was several miles from his own home, and then he had the stamina to run the rest of the way.

He was out of breath, finally catching up with his elder brother Samir at Basim's farmhouse. Nazar was running down the dirt road leading to the farm. In the distance, he saw the simple white stucco farmhouse next to the old wooden barn, and then Samir frantically packing up Basim's truck with luggage, bags, boxes, and satchels.

Basim's place was in the direction of Mosul, towards the west. It was situated right in the middle of isolated farm terrain, where flat and seemingly endless wheat fields spread out in all directions. Under normal circumstances, Nazar cherished this farm as a place of family memories, serenity, laughter, and great food. Basim was his favourite uncle as well as a true friend to Baba. Both Nazar and Samir had enjoyed helping Basim for many seasons over the years, especially when it came time to plant or harvest his crops. Then they always would look forward to the tradition of celebrating with their cousins when the work was done.

It was almost sunset. The vast cloudless sky of the Nineveh plains had become a bright pink. The sun was an enormous orange ball rapidly lowering toward the horizon.

The beauty of nature did not disguise the anxiety and tension which Samir wore on his face. When Samir stared at him, Nazar felt it like a knife in his gut.

Samir was angry and yelled at Nazar as he got closer to the truck, "What are you doing here, Nazar? Baba left you a note this morning. He said that you were to stay at the home and do the routine farming work and then wait for us to return. I saw the note. He wrote in big letters: NAZAR—STAY HOME, FEED THE CHICKENS AND THE REST OF THE ANIMALS, DO ALL YOUR CHORES AND WAIT HERE. DO NOT LEAVE THE FARM. WE WILL BE BACK LATER TODAY. WAIT FOR US. You can read, Nazar! You can read better than me. How could you do this to us?"

"But Samir…it was getting dark…no one called the house…no one stopped by. I could not reach anyone when I tried the phone. It was very quiet. It was too quiet. I was getting worried. Then I heard explosions outside in the distance. I couldn't even trick myself into believing it was another one of our violent summer storms. I could not wait any longer, Samir."

"Nazar, it is dangerous here. Very dangerous. Look at the horizon. Can you see those shadows? They may look so little from here—almost like grasshoppers, but those are tanks moving east from Mosul. They are enemy tanks. Some of them are moving quickly in our direction—and—I know you don't understand anything about this—but I have to help Basim get out of here with his stuff before they arrive… How did you know I was here?"

"I was half asleep this morning when I heard you and Baba talking…and I remember him telling you something about helping out Uncle Basim."

"Nazar, you are clever—but this was a stupid move! Look at those tanks—can you see that maybe one or two of them are headed our way, maybe right now, you have to get out of here immediately. And they are likely rumbling towards us through the fields—along with those evil warriors prowling around with their RPGs and their rifles. You need to get back home, Nazar."

Samir was thinking quickly. He looked around and noticed there was a small beat-up Chinese made motorbike parked near the house.

Just then, Basim walked out of the house with more bundles in his arms. He was a tall, healthy, robust man with an unkempt beard. He exuded energy and determination, but he was suddenly shocked to see Nazar, "Nazar, what are you doing here! This is terrible! You must get out of here immediately…I can't take you in our truck. It is all packed up and I don't have the time to even make room for you. I am headed to Ankawa. You need to get back to your father's house. I am leaving in just a few minutes. Samir, look over there towards the horizon. Can you see what I am seeing? There are militants nearby and they will not be friendly with us. This is getting dangerous, why don't you take him away in your small Nissan and just go?" Samir replied, "No Uncle Basim, I won't be leaving until I see that you are on the road to Ankawa. That is what Baba insisted, but I taught Nazar how to use a motorbike." He pointed to the one nearby the house, "Does this one work? Does it have gas in it? Uncle, could he drive it to our home? We will get it back to you later someday soon when things are back to normal."

Basim replied, "Samir, we cannot fit the motorbike into the truck. I may never see it again. Yes, Nazar, take it immediately and drive it back home. It has enough gas to get you there. It is ugly and it rattles, but it works. Right away, please. Samir will be following right after you in his Nissan. Just give us a few more minutes."

Nazar protested, "I can help you finish up, Uncle. Also, can I go inside to say goodbye to Aunt Miriam and the cousins?"

"No," Basim said sternly, "Aunt Miriam and your cousins are already with other Christians in Ankawa. Perhaps you know the route, Nazar? It is east of here—in the city of Erbil. They were away visiting with her family well before all this trouble came upon us. You must get out of here immediately. I am sorry. You will understand later."

Nazar sadly gave his brother Samir and his uncle a quick hug and obediently went to the motorbike, turned on the ignition, and travelled down the dirt road away from the farmhouse. Using the motorbike was effortless for him as Samir had taught him well. At the end of the dirt road, he turned around and looked back at Samir and his beloved Uncle Basim, who were talking excitedly to each other and waving their arms.

Nazar gazed at them one last time, then sped down the larger paved road to head home. Within seconds he suddenly heard several explosions of mortars or grenades in the fields—right in the vicinity of Basim's farmhouse! He thought he also heard a barrage of bullets somewhere. He had heard bullets before, but never this close by. They sounded like fireworks, but louder and more threatening. No, those sounds were not fireworks! He knew they were all in great danger. He circled back to the beginning of the dirt road leading to his uncle's place.

Samir and Basim saw him in the distance. Samir yelled, "Get out of here! Move fast, Nazar!"

Nazar was almost frozen in place, mesmerised by what he was witnessing at the farmhouse from his distant vantage point.

Seemingly out of nowhere, an enormous shiny Abrams tank appeared and rapidly approached the property. It was one of those tanks stolen by the enemy fighters, with its harsh, grating sounds created by the huge rumbling wheels and treads. There was an additional series of explosions in the fields surrounding the farmhouse. Nazar could not tell whether they were coming from a mortar or an RPG. He knew nothing about weapons of war as his father told him nothing about them, nor did his father ever talk about the deadly machines of war. He could not see warriors, nor could he see what they were aiming at. Every time there was an explosion, dark smoke and dust billowed into the air.

Then Nazar saw the side view of the Abrams tank pivoting and aiming directly at Basim's truck! Samir and Basim looked stunned, unable to determine whether they could still escape the danger. They crouched down next to Basim's truck, hoping to shield themselves from bullets.

The tank fired once from the end of its huge gun. The ground shook underneath Nazar and almost threw him off his bike. He noticed a large flaming spark as the shot was detonated. Then, in an instant, there was a massive explosion right where Basim's truck was parked, then a second deafening explosion, which Nazar feared might be the gas tank of Samir's small Nissan nearby.

Samir and Basim had vanished before his eyes.

Clouds of dust, plumes of black smoke, and blazing red fire were everywhere. Then, within seconds, the fire was spreading to the roof of Basim's farmhouse.

Paralysed in fear, Nazar called out, "Samir! Basim!"
But no one answered.

Nazar was shocked and terrified. There was no doubt in his mind that he had just lost two of his most treasured friends. His blood was burning with anger. He wanted to yell, to scream, to cry, to collapse—all at the same time. He raised his fists in the air and shouted out a cry of grief to the skies.

But his angry blood was also invigorated with fresh adrenalin. He knew he had to get moving. He knew he was seconds away from the same horror happening to him. He did not look back any longer. He sped away on the motorbike faster than the wind.

He did not return to his own farmhouse, as Samir had insisted. He fled instead towards the village of Karemlesh as the sun was descending below the horizon into a dreary smoky haze.

The endless, cruel nightmare had continued as Nazar remained sleeping at the edge of the dusty road, right in the middle of the village. His heart was beating faster and faster. His wounded arm began to throb with pain. The hurt felt like a knife piercing inside him.

Suddenly his nightmare transported him to the top of the bell tower of the church of Mar Addai. Deacon Sermed, the old sacristan with a long white beard, was frantically pulling on the rope to ring the enormous bells, and they began to chime loudly. At first, Nazar thought that the deep and rich sounds coming from the huge bells were summoning the people of Karemlesh to the morning Mass. He knew that Sermed would vigorously and zealously pull the ropes every morning without fail. But when he saw the apprehension on the deacon's face, Nazar knew the bells were being rung to signal an emergency. Anyone in the immediate vicinity of Mar Addai would not escape the overpowering resonance of those bells.

So it was that the frantically ringing church bells of his dream abruptly awakened Nazar, as if he were listening to real physical sounds with his ears. The bells had liberated him at last from the terrors and torture of his nightmare.

Mar Addai

Once Nazar rubbed and opened his eyes, he became aware that he had been dreaming. His left ear was ringing, and he swatted the side of his head to see if he could get rid of the strange sounds, but they would not go away. He was staring up at the bell tower and noticed that the bells were not moving and were absolutely silent. Perhaps there was no deacon to ring the bells? Maybe there was no priest to say Mass, and no people to attend? Could the entire village of Karemlesh be empty?

He realised that he didn't just experience one of his typical frightening dreams that he could shake off with the morning sunlight. It really happened—all of it. His nightmare had viciously and unrelentingly replayed all the terrible and traumatic memories of the day before.

His head was pounding and aching as he sat up. The August sun was intense, bright as in the peak of summer, and the intensity made his eyes squint. He looked around and realised he was sitting in the dirty street. He saw the blood where something sharp had grazed the side of his arm. He concluded that he must have collapsed in the darkness—when he was overcome by the crowds of frightened people running in the night. He remembered a very loud explosion and falling debris. Maybe that's when he fell to the ground? He touched the top of his head and he felt a bruise but no cut. He was relieved that, miraculously, nothing seemed to be lodged in his arm—but there was a gash.

He struggled to get up from the ground. Once he was standing, the first thought that came to him was, *Baba. Where was he?*

A feeling of indescribable fear and loneliness swept over him.

As his senses reawakened, he smelled the stench of burning wood and rubber in the air. Patches of smoke filled the streets like a fog. There was a crater in the road not too far from where he was standing.

His eyes searched for the old men who liked to chat in front of their shops; for the young women who hurried down the street towards the marketplace to buy their fruit and meat; for the crows, dogs, cats and chickens who wandered aimlessly in the road and always got in the way of the cars, and for the children laughing and the adults fretting as they walked hurriedly on their way to work.

But there was nothing, no cars, no people, no animals.

His eyes looked down at the ground with deep sadness.

Then something—or possibly someone—made him look up. There, right across the street, he recognised the entrance of Mar Addai, the church dedicated to St Thaddeus. It was not the same beautiful church which cheerfully welcomed the crowds as they hurried up the steps to Mass. Now it was desolate and abandoned. As he looked across the street at the courtyard outside the church entrance, he noticed that the tall, massive wooden front doors of the church were smashed open and hanging loosely from their hinges, creaking in the morning breeze as they swung back and forth.

He stumbled across the street in a daze, almost as if he was being called inside. Nazar dusted off his pants, walked into the courtyard, then up the steps of the church and went in.

The magnificent deep-blue stained-glass church windows were now shattered with holes in them, letting in rays of daylight. There was a smell of burning wood in the air. Ceiling beams were hanging down—and in other places, there were big gaps in the roof. Bullet marks could be seen on the pillars and walls. A few splotches of blood were on the marble floor which once had a magnificent shine, but no more. The ceiling seemed blackened in places, perhaps because someone had tried to set the church on fire, or perhaps because of explosions from grenades.

This was all a terrible shock to Nazar. As he walked farther into the church, all he could see was destruction, with the altar battered and the pulpit thrown over.

Engraved on the wall directly in back of the pulpit, there were words in Aramaic which quoted a verse from the gospel of Matthew: *This is my beloved Son, with whom I am well pleased*. Nazar was shocked to see that the words *beloved Son* appeared to have been beaten and disfigured with a hammer, and, in addition, were marred with black spray paint. A great heaviness and dread came upon him as he surveyed all the evidence of sacrilege.

But what about the statue of the Virgin Mary with the smiling face? Where was she? She was Nazar's favourite, with her kind brown eyes that looked right at him. After his mother died, when he was only eight years old, he and Baba would stop after Mass at the shrine of the Virgin each week to light a candle and ask for her help for the family. Nazar remembered how his own mother used to hold him tightly in her arms when he was little, singing beautiful melodies to him before putting him to bed. She sang even more beautifully than the Skylark. Whenever he lit his candle at the shrine and looked up at the serene face of the woman, he imagined the statue coming alive, with Mary wrapping her arms around Nazar and holding him tightly—just like his mother used to do.

I must look for her, thought Nazar, *She must be frightened.*

There was a pile of boards, prayer books, scattered pages of organ music, splinters of wood, nails and toppled-over chairs nearby. And, at last, he found the statue—under a large pile of debris. Nazar tossed the boards away with angry determination. His arm ached, but nothing would stop him.

How could they do this to her, he thought.

The statue of the Virgin had fallen flat on her back onto the church floor. Her head was separated from the rest of her body. Nazar looked closely and could see a smooth clean cut above the neck of the statue. Could someone have cut off her head with a sharp sword or knife? Then he saw that her hands were missing. He looked around but they were nowhere to be found. When he touched the rough edges of stone where her two hands used to be, Nazar could once again detect the smooth clean cut. Then he knew for sure. Someone had fiercely cut off both the head and hands of his treasured statue! *Maybe they used a big sword,* he thought, *how could they have such hatred? And for her? For Mary, the mother of Jesus? This beautiful kind woman who brings the joy of heaven into our world!* Then, not believing the sacrilege his eyes were witnessing, Nazar knelt on the cold stone floor of the church and kissed her, while his tears poured down and washed her face.

It was all too much for the young man to bear. Nazar began to weep deeply and then clenched his hands in anger and despair.

For a few moments, it was quiet in the church. Nazar was suddenly calm. The persistent ringing in his ear had stopped. Birds were singing outside. The Skylark peered in through the broken window.

In the stillness, Nazar heard a gentle voice—the voice of a woman. He turned around to see if anyone was there, but the church was empty.

He looked down at the face of the Mary.

The voice said, "Nazar, I have no hands to give away my love. Without my hands I cannot give away my love. Nazar, will you be my hands?"

There was no doubt in Nazar's mind that the message came from the statue. Surprisingly, he was not at all alarmed.

"Yes, I will try," replied Nazar out loud in the echoing church, and nodded courageously, "I will do my best. I promise." Then he made a little cross over the forehead of the woman and kissed her cheek.

Nazar knelt on the floor for a few minutes in silence, then he suddenly got very drowsy and searched for a place in the church to rest. The pews were covered in dust and debris, so he wandered into the sacristy where the priests put on their vestments. Nazar knew the room because he had been an altar boy only a few years ago. He saw a bench along the wall, stretched out on it and fell fast asleep.

In about an hour something prompted him to sit up. He rubbed his eyes and stared directly in front of him at a cracked mirror hanging from the wall. He stumbled off the bench towards the mirror. He was shocked to see his tanned handsome face all covered with dirt. His curly dark brown hair was sprinkled with dust and debris from the street. His right cheek was bruised. He saw his muscular arms—and then the blood splotched over his shirt from the wound in his arm. He touched the wound and was alarmed. He became aware that he was still alive, and took a deep breath just to prove to himself that he was able to breathe. Then he stepped forward closer to the mirror, to show he could still walk. The face he gazed at in the mirror was exhausted, dazed, and very downcast.

He turned away from the mirror and left the sacristy. He suddenly felt his empty stomach growling and decided to go outside the church and see if he could find something to eat. He looked one more time at the broken statue, wondering whether he really had heard her speak, then went out the battered doors.

Amira and Yousif

As soon as he walked down the church steps, Nazar heard the voice of a middle-aged woman calling out to him from the side of the building. He peered around the corner. "Please come with me, I need your help. I have no one to help me," she beckoned to Nazar with her hands, "Come with me, please."

Nazar looked carefully at the woman's face. Her hair was partially grey. Her hazel eyes had kindness and wisdom in them—like the deep waters of the ocean. She had a few wrinkles of age, but in her agitation, and with her arms waving, she seemed to have the abundant energy of youth. Her sense of urgency wasn't in any way disturbing or troubling to Nazar, as he could only perceive goodness and compassion radiating from her face. Nazar recognised a beauty in her countenance, a beauty which any artist would be challenged to depict. It was an inner beauty, perhaps emanating from the depths of her soul, a beauty which endures and even flourishes with the passage of time.

"I prayed to the good Lord for help," she said, "and I was told my prayer was about to be answered, so I wondered what to do, then I left the house to look around, and see…here you are—my answer. You look strong. I think you are big enough...but...what's this?" She noticed the blood on his torn shirt, "You are hurt! Come with me to my house and I will bandage that arm. Are you hungry? I have a little food left in my kitchen. And then, after you rest a little...I am hoping you will be able to help me."

They walked together down the alley next to the church, towards the neighbourhood with all the small houses. This wasn't too far from where Nazar used to go to school. There was a very narrow street that they went into, too narrow for a car to get through, and they stopped at a grey stone building with small windows and a red door with a big N written on it—splashed in black paint. The woman took out her key and opened the door and they went inside.

"Here is my problem..." she said, leading Nazar into a room in the back of the house. Nazar noticed that the house was simply furnished—clean and tidy, just like his own farmhouse outside of the village. They went into a bedroom and there was an older man with white hair and tanned skin, sitting up in the bed. He was awake and alert, and as the woman walked into the room, he smiled with serenity.

"Father, I don't know how it happened—look at this strong young man. I asked for help and God has sent him to us." She went closer to her father and kissed him, and her father took Nazar's hand and looked up at him, "Maybe he is an angel," he said quietly.

Then they left the bedroom and walked towards the kitchen, "This is my problem," said the woman, "he is my problem—my father. Well, I should also say he is my joy, forgive me. I do not want anything to happen to him. As you might have noticed, his leg has been injured so he can no longer walk, at least not for a few weeks I suspect. He is a builder. Just like St Joseph. That's his name, you know—Yousif. And you know what? That was my grandfather's name—and my great grandfather's too, all builders. Over the years they must have built half of the village. He works mostly with stone, cinder blocks, and concrete. As you can see, he is short and thin, always on his feet—he is very strong. It was just the other day he fell off a ladder! I have not been able to get him to a doctor yet…so we were hoping that resting on his back, would heal the problem with his leg. So far that hasn't worked. Maybe he has a fracture, maybe a bruise or a torn ligament. I am usually pretty good at figuring out if someone has a broken bone. I hope he doesn't. Either way, he will need time to recover. But we have no time with the dark storm which has burst upon us. Thank God, his mind is perfect. No head injury. But he can't walk on that leg.

"I did not want to leave him here, although the crowds have been rushing out of the city for the last two days. My friends begged me to go with them, but I refused. Looks to me like everyone has gone. I cannot leave him here.

"Those cruel men waving their rifles and their dark flags will be here soon. When they see the N on the door, we will all be in great danger."

Nazar looked at her with a troubled expression. He had noticed the N splashed with black paint on the front door, but no one told him what it meant.

She continued, "The N means Nazarene. We are Christians. It is because we are followers of Jesus.

"I think there were two of them—you know, the men who wave the flags with the skull and wear the dark masks over their faces to hide their eyes. My friends told me there were two strangers walking down this street the other day, and these men were questioning the neighbours quietly. I am guessing that they are the ones who must have painted the N on our door. They could have been the evil warriors in disguise—unless it was someone else from town who was being threatened to follow their orders? What a terrible thought. They will come back here sooner or later. I am sure of that. My father is well known in Karemlesh. Perhaps that is why the door was painted with the N. They will force my father to say that he is *not* a Christian, and—I know him all too well—he will stubbornly say that he *is* a Christian, and then maybe they will beat him and maybe even kill him. If I am here, I do not want to tell you what they will do to me. So, I must try to get him out of this house…but I cannot do it by myself, as you can see."

She looked into Nazar's eyes and suddenly changed her tone from worry about her predicament to concern for the young man who had suddenly entered their lives, "But let us not do anything yet. I need to get you something to eat and bandage your arm, which I suppose was cut by a piece of metal or shrapnel flying in the air with the explosions last night. Am I right? It is a good thing it did not get into your eye—or your brain. There is so much injury and destruction all around us. Let me look at that cut. As far as I can tell there is no metal piece still lodged in there. I will put my special ointment on it and wrap up your arm."

Amira went to her cabinet, took out her salve and bandages, and went to work on the wounded arm, "It may continue to hurt but—the arm is not broken….and you look strong and healthy, so time will heal it, no doubt. You know, I do see a pretty big bump on the top of your head, but no cut.

We could put some ice on that...Young man, I think you might really be the answer to my prayer."

Nazar responded, "Yes, I am. I am strong, I help my father on the farm after school and whenever I have free time. I lift and move the heavy soil for planting with my shovel, I clean out the barns, I feed the animals and do all the same chores my father does. I don't have much time to play with friends, but when I do, we go to the fields and kick the soccer ball around."

"How old are you?"

"I am 13. In November, I will be 14. I have muscles on my arms."

"Yes, I see that. I will need to ask your mother and father if it is OK for you to go with me. Where is your family now—your mother and your father?"

"My mother was very sick with a terrible illness a few years ago and she died. Something was not good in her blood. I was eight then. My father," Nazar paused and controlled his feeling of dread, "Baba was missing all day yesterday. Aram said he could have been helping some elderly people from the village—then there were the explosions and everyone running from the centre of the town—I do not know where he is now.

"And my brother Samir disappeared in a horrible explosion at Uncle Basim's farm. It happened just yesterday at sunset. And my uncle too is gone..."

He began to cry for a few moments, then fell silent. He broke the silence and altered his feelings with the words, "See, I am strong. I can help you."

"I know this must be very frightening for you. It is also frightening for me. This is a terrible tragedy you have witnessed. Your brother Samir is gone! And your uncle? It doesn't seem possible—just yesterday? It is horrible—but I see you are a brave young man. Maybe your father is helping someone else now and will catch up with you later once everything is calm. There are so many people who desperately need help. Let us hope that your father is not harmed. Is it possible that I could have met him at the church? If I am right, he is a very good man. Perhaps he is the man who is short and has a moustache, no? Strong arms, kind brown eyes, and a very tanned face with wrinkles, almost like leather. He looks a bit like you. He has the face of someone who works outside in the wheat fields. And I think he raises chickens, because he is always helping people at the parish and in the town, giving away the eggs. He always kept saying he had too many eggs. Am I right? Perhaps I have even worked with him at the soup kitchen, preparing food for the needy... The more I think about it, I would not be surprised if your father were helping some elderly and disabled people to escape from the village yesterday morning. He is probably still with them, and once he is sure they are safe, I think he will be searching for you."

Amira put some lentil soup and bread out on the kitchen table and Nazar began to devour everything quickly. He was famished. Amira sat down next to him, "How is my cooking? I know it is hot outside, and here I am serving you hot lentil soup, but it will comfort you. My father loves it."

"Yes, it is very good, thank you."

"And what is your name? I am sorry I was so preoccupied. I should have asked you when we met."

"Nazar."

"Nazar? Let me look at you. I do know several Nazars in the town. There are many of them. By any chance were you one of the children I prepared for first communion when you were seven?"

"Yes, I was seven when I received my first communion here at Mar Addai. The woman who prepared me and my friends had a beautiful first name, let me think, A-mir—I know, it was Amira. Now I remember."

"Well, that is my name, so I must be the one who prepared you for that beautiful day."

"And you told us then that Amira means princess. I remember that."

"Yes, it does, you have a good memory. My father wanted me to have that name. He used to call me his little princess, maybe he was thinking of a lovely Arabian princess—although, I must admit, I don't feel like much of a princess these days. And now you are almost 14, Nazar. Is that right? Let me look at you. You have grown and changed so much since you were seven. I honestly did not recognise you when I was calling for help. Please forgive me. You have such long legs now, the legs of a runner. Your face has become so handsome and mature…And I guess I have changed too, gotten some grey hairs and wrinkles since those days. The suffering of war has aged me, Nazar. But we are both older and wiser now, don't you think? Do you know what your name means?"

"Well, maybe, something to do with Nazareth."

"And who came from Nazareth?"

"Jesus?"

"Yes, exactly. You are a Nazarene, a follower of Jesus. A disciple."

"Like the N on the door."

"Yes, to have that name is a great honour and dignity, Nazar. It is nothing to hide from. We must let our dignity shine out like a burning torch to every person we meet. Your father and mother had high hopes for you when they gave you that name...Well, Nazar, we have been talking a lot and you need to eat some more and then rest a while—so let's see what else I can give you from the kitchen. There is no more lentil soup left, but I have some lamb stew. I will heat it up now. Do you like lamb?"

"Yes, of course. Everyone loves lamb."

"OK. You'll have some lamb stew and then rest at least a little while—and then—we can plan our journey."

"Our journey?"

While she put the stew on the stove and more leftover bread in the oven, she told Nazar about her plan, "Well, first of all, I have to show you what I did yesterday while everyone was running away. Do you see what this is?" She pointed to her unfinished project—two broomsticks attached with some rope to a sturdy folded tablecloth, "I am going to make something we can use to carry my father. I put two broomsticks on each side of the cloth, and we will finish attaching it to the broomsticks with my strong rope—we will have a stretcher, you know, just like in the old war movies. Perhaps you are too young for the war movies? My father and I are always watching them. We like to see the heroes win.

"And I will take one side and you will take the other and we can carry him out of the house."

"Yes, we could do it—as long as he is not very heavy—but I really don't think he is heavy—he looks so thin to me. On the other hand, I see he has a lot of muscles. That would make him heavier. I think we can both carry him, Amira, for a short journey—but not for miles."

"Yes, only for a short journey. To the main road that goes to Erbil. My sister Zara runs a clinic in the Christian district of the town—almost like a small hospital, in Erbil. We can bring him there...As long as we can get there safely...Do you know something? She is a religious sister, a nun, and here I am still calling her Zara. She is a Dominican. Have you seen them? They wear the black and white habits. Those sisters in Erbil are all Iraqi. They are not the nuns from Europe. They care for our sick and wounded. They will take anyone who is sick, rich or poor, Christian or Muslim. You know, Nazar, funny thing, I still call her Zara—I like to call her Zara—because she has always been my dear Zara, my elder sister...We played together and grew up together. We'd steal each other's jewellery and clothes and shoes so we could dress up and go out, then we'd fight about it. 'You took my necklace! You took my shoes!' And then we'd make up afterwards. We laughed and cried together. We laughed when we played tricks on the boys. We cried when our mother died. She is my dear Zara. But there, in the city, they call her Sister Caterina. She is the mother superior of the order located in Erbil, and she runs the clinic."

Amira put the heated lamb stew and more bread on the table for Nazar to devour.

"Ca-ter-ina?" he said hesitantly.

"That's Italian for Catherine. She is named after St Catherine of Siena, in Italy, who cared for the sick during the plague—you know, the black death—this was in the Medieval period, maybe seven hundred years ago. I could tell you much more about St Catherine, but not now. The main thing is, just remember, when you see her, call her Sister Caterina."

"We live in Iraq. We are not in Italy. Why Cat-er-ina?" This time, he had the pronunciation just right.

"You said that perfectly, Nazar. Zara was a very good student. She went to the University of Baghdad and then became a scholar of languages—a linguist. She was brilliant. She taught there for many years too. She knew Latin, Greek, and even Hebrew. And she knew all about ancient Aramaic, which is where the language we are speaking now—Sureth—comes from. Think about it, Nazar—the language that you and I are speaking right now is the same language Jesus spoke when he walked the face of the earth."

"I didn't know that, Amira."

"Then, you know what? Something amazing happened to her. She told me she fell in love with the Lord. Those were her very words. At first, I was puzzled. Then I knew it was real. She was different, Nazar. She was joyful and radiant. She still is. She was always a happy person, but this was different. She told me she was going to leave everything behind. She said she wanted to possess the pearl of great price. That's what she said to me."

"What pearl? I don't understand."

"Jesus…He is the pearl of great price. She is right, you know. With so much death and destruction happening all around us, I don't want to frighten you…but you already know what I am talking about—with so many people we know, friends and family and others, having to abandon everything they own and worked for—in the end, He is all that really matters. That's the way she sees it, and she is right. He is the pearl. Knowing that we are loved by Him, having Him, is everything."

Nazar was silent. Her way of looking at life was all too profound for him to grasp.

Amira continued, "Zara went through a stunning change, no doubt about it, Nazar. She even said she was willing to die for the Lord, she loved Him so much. So that is the true reason why she became a Dominican nun. And they call her Sister Caterina."

Amira smiled, "You want to hear something else, Nazar? Here she knows all these ancient languages, but she tells me she loves Italian and French the most. She is the one who kept repeating the phrase in French, '*Le bon Dieu*,' when she would counsel me to stay calm and not to worry. At first, I didn't know what she was talking about, until she told me it meant 'the good God.' Then, I translated it to 'the good Lord' in our language. So, once she taught me that expression, I never stopped using it. *The good Lord.* Isn't that beautiful? My friends hear me saying it all the time. I suspect they are tired of me saying it, but they don't let on."

"Yes, it is nice—but don't you think we should try to figure out what we should do about your father, Amira? Why don't we try to get into Mosul—it is a big city with lots of people. I have been there with Baba. Mosul must have an excellent hospital with many nurses and doctors. We would just have to find a way to hide and get around those tanks—the ones I saw in the distance when I was at Uncle Basim's farm."

"Tanks! You saw tanks. Those would be enemy tanks, no doubt. The Abrams tanks taken over by the militants! I understand you are in some ways still a boy, Nazar. I do not think you know about all the terrible things that have happened in Mosul. Perhaps your father has tried to protect you, keeping you at peace in our once quiet town, working each day at the farm, and letting you play ball with your friends. Maybe he has not told you about Mosul. I think he must have tried for as long as possible to allow you to grow up as a happy young man without the fear and terror that has now come upon us. The city of Mosul—the entire city—Nazar, has been destroyed by an army of cruel men who call themselves warriors. But they are cowards. They want to force us to accept their distorted ideology by using the weapons of fear and violence. I won't dignify it by calling it a religion. It is their excuse to act with hatred and revenge towards anyone who will not adhere to their way of thinking.

"All the Christians—and countless Muslims—who survived, have fled from that city in great anxiety. And the same thing has just happened to our town. Beautiful buildings and homes are all empty now. I shudder to think about what they will do to the Church of Mar Addai—I see in your face that you know more than you are telling me. You were inside the church, weren't you? Please don't tell me what you saw. I could not bear it. And what has happened to your father? It is a great evil which has smothered us, Nazar—like dark clouds choking our blue summer sky. No, we cannot go to Mosul. Mosul is no longer. We must go east to Erbil. That is where Zara is."

Nazar finished up his stew and bread and was lost in thought, "Amira, you said Zara again. You mean, Sister Caterina, don't you? But I do not understand about the N on the door. My friend Rafiq is not a Christian. We play soccer together all the time, and I even invited him to come to Mass with me one Sunday with Baba. He saw everything that goes on in our church. We sat in the back so no one would notice him and ask him questions. I even showed him the statue of the Virgin. He lit a candle there with me."

Nazar began to recount a vivid memory of a special time with his friend. "And do you know that Rafiq invited me to go with his whole family to Bartella. There were eight of us in the car! We were all stuffed in but we laughed. When we arrived at the big mosque, you know, the one in the town with the tall tower. They put a prayer robe on me, and snuck me in with them. I can't remember the name of that mosque, but anyway, it was crowded—I took off my shoes, took my place on the carpet with the others, I bowed, I pretended to say the prayers, I didn't know any of them—it was very serious, very—I am looking for a word to tell you what it was like—I was surrounded in front and back of me by men kneeling and bowing. There was a beautiful smell in the air, like the fresh air of the wheat fields."

"*Solemn*, that is the word you are looking for. It means their prayers were sincere, and I believe Someone was listening."

"Yes, it was solemn—I remember. For me, the chanting was almost scary, like something out of a strange dream. You know what I mean, Amira, you must have heard the chanting from the minaret in Bartella, or maybe somewhere else. Anyway, as I was saying, Rafiq and I have always been friends. He has never said or done anything to me to hurt me. We joked, we laughed, we teased the girls. We are great friends. Although, now I am trying to think back—it is strange that I have not seen him in the last week—I do not understand about the N on your door, Amira. I don't see why—the warriors you are talking about—why they want to hurt Christians."

Then Nazar came to a sudden realisation and became agitated, "Amira, I don't want to tell you this, I don't want to add to your trouble, but now I am thinking about the tank which fired on Uncle Basim and Samir—and the explosions yesterday. Uncle Basim was very proud of his faith. Do you know that a few years ago he made a large wooden cross and put it up on the side of his barn? He wanted everyone to know that he was proud of being a Christian. He said to me that Christians should never forget their—dignity. That was his word. *Dignity*. I remembered it, Amira. Yes, I still remember it. Maybe the warriors driving that tank saw the wooden cross! Maybe that's why they fired at him." He looked up at Amira with an expression of pain and disbelief, "Why such hatred? And why do they hate Mary?"

"I wish I had the time now to explain, Nazar. You have been sheltered from much of the evil that has been overtaking our homeland. It is as if the dark storm clouds are moving in quickly, and all the trees are shaking in the wind. You rest now for a few hours, and I will get my father ready to leave. We don't have much time, but the good Lord will give us the time we need."

"Yes, the good Lord, *Le Bon Dieu*."

"Nazar, you said that just right. It sounded like perfect French. You are a quick learner. Seriously, let's do some planning. We cannot carry much with us. I will bring some food and supplies, and we will put it all in a backpack."

"I will carry the backpack. I am strong, and I will carry the stretcher with you too."

After he finished eating, Amira showed Nazar a cot she had available, and, at her suggestion, he stretched out on the cot and took a nap. Meanwhile, she helped Yousif get dressed and ready to leave the house. Then she finished up her homemade invention with the broomsticks and folded sheet, deciding to leave a few knots untied for Nazar to attend to when he woke up.

It was not long before Nazar was wide awake, "Amira, when do you want to leave for the journey?"

"We can leave very soon. Almost everything is ready. While you were sleeping, my father and I ate a big lunch. We tried to use up as much food as we could so it wouldn't spoil while we are away. I left a few knots for you to finish for me, and then my stretcher will be all set."

"Yes, I will do the knots, I can do four or five if you want, I can even tie them without looking. I can tie them behind my back. That was another thing my father taught me."

"Nazar, you are a gift from heaven. Now we are almost done. We can bring a little water with us in a jug, but not too much because water is heavy, and we have enough to carry. Here is your backpack. Also, I have a backpack with some clothes and medicines and other things which I can take. If we can find a stream with clean water on our way, or maybe a well, we can get more water as we go along."

"My Baba says to me to drink a lot of water in the summer when I am working outside at the farm. This is still mid-August, so we must drink a lot of water, Amira. And it is not good for us to be out in the hot sun in the middle of the day."

"Well, let us try to go for an hour and maybe an hour and a half if we can. That will bring us to noon. Maybe then we can try to find some shade and eat a bit and rest before we continue on."

"Where did you say we are going? Was it Erbil? I have never been there. I think that's too far away to walk."

"Yes, I completely agree, Nazar. Erbil is too far away for us to walk. Still, I saw hundreds of villagers fleeing Karemlesh yesterday, and also the day before yesterday. Almost all of them were on foot. No doubt it will be a painful and dangerous journey for them. Perhaps for us as well. I suppose in a perfect world, my father would have driven us today in his work vehicle. But with that injured leg, it is out of the question. And do you know, Nazar, that all my life I have never driven? I do all my errands right here in town on foot. Anytime I need to travel outside the village, my father or a friend will drive me.

"So, we will start out in Karemlesh, walking quietly and carefully through the narrow streets. I know this part of town perfectly. It is like a maze. We don't want to be seen so we will only be for a little while in the centre of the village. If the cruel warriors return, we must not be seen, you understand? We are going to try to get ourselves safely to the main road that goes to Erbil. If a good Samaritan comes our way with a truck or van, we will ask for their help to get us all to Erbil, including my father, of course. I want him to be safe. While you were sleeping, would you believe it? He kept saying it was OK to leave him behind, but I won't do that, Nazar.

"If the evil warriors find us before we find the good Samaritan, it will be a terrible thing. We could be harmed, Nazar, so you must be very brave. I don't want to think about it now."

"The Good Samaritan?" Nazar thought for a while. "Oh, I understand, he was the man who was traveling along the road in the story. The Good Samaritan noticed the injured man who was left lying in the road, almost dead, beaten by robbers. And then, he didn't just *notice*, Amira. He *stopped* and helped the man. Then he brought him—let's see if I can remember—yes, he brought him to an inn, and the innkeeper took care of him and healed him."

"Yes, said Amira. That is exactly the lesson of the parable. You got it right."

Nazar continued, absorbed in thought, "So, you need someone like that to help us accomplish our journey. But Amira, what if he never shows up when we need him? What if people pass us by and don't stop to help, just like they did to that poor fellow? I think they will be too frightened to stop."

"I don't want to think about it. We cannot let fear stop us, Nazar. Every step we take, every breath we breathe is a gift of God. We will let the good Lord carry us when we have no more strength left on our own. Just think about it that way. He will not let us down. We will go to the clinic where Zara is, there I go again, you know, Sister Caterina, and we will be safe. Then we can also see if there is some way to locate your father."

The rest of the preparations all went quickly—the knots were tied, Amira's father fit perfectly in the stretcher, Amira had her backpack, Nazar had his backpack, and the jug of water was attached to Nazar's belt so his hands could be free. He was at the front of the stretcher and Amira was at the back. They went out the door, locked it, and Amira made a sign of the cross over the home before they turned and went down the narrow street.

By Paths They Have Not Known I Will Guide Them

There were alley ways, narrow streets that were only wide enough for a small cart; there were wider streets that cars could travel on, but it was exactly like Amira said—a very complicated maze. Amira knew when to turn right and left, when to pause and take a drink of water in the shade of the concrete buildings, when to stop and listen for sounds of activity. There was damage to the houses, broken windows, stones and loose bricks in the road, and they had to watch where they were walking so as not to trip and hurt Amira's father. As they travelled, he never complained, just quietly said some prayers, and he looked up at Nazar from time to time with his shining, affirming eyes.

It was only an hour or so before they arrived closer to the centre of Karemlesh. They were approaching the wider street with all the busy shops and the cars coming and going, except that on this day there was no activity.

"We need to cross this street, Nazar. I will wait here with my father. You go very carefully to the corner and look out in both directions. Make sure there is no one there to see us. I am hoping the cruel fighters are not back yet."

Nazar followed her instructions, looking to the right and to the left. When he looked to the left, he was stunned to see the massive slabs of concrete which had fallen into the street, the collapsed roofs, dangling electrical wires, cars burned and turned upside down and others abandoned, stones and bricks and large pieces of metal strewn everywhere. There was no one walking on the main street, no one at the markets. For a few moments, all was a deadly quiet. There was a stench of burning rubber in the summer air.

Then Nazar looked to the right. He could hear the sound of engines rumbling, growing louder and approaching the centre of the town. As he squinted his eyes looking into the distance, he saw a jeep and two trucks loaded with young men getting closer and closer, with the sound of their vehicles roaring like angry lions. They had masks on their faces and turbans on their heads, and they were tightly holding the flags with the skull painted on them. They were shouting out slogans and seemed to be boasting about their conquest of the village. And they were waving their guns in the air. Nazar had seen those long deadly rifles in some movies and on TV. A chill went down his spine. It was the evil fighters, passing right in front of him down the main street of Karemlesh!

The first thought that came to Nazar was that he must swallow hard and hide his fear from Amira and her father. He quickly walked back to them as they waited in the shade, and without any indication of panic in his speech, he told them about the fighters.

"Maybe if we are patient and wait a while, they will pass down the street and then we can cross to the other side. I don't see anyone or anything, so I think this will work. I will go back and keep a look out, and I will let you know as soon as it looks safe. You just stay in the shade and drink more water. I will be back soon."

Amira and her father looked at each other, impressed by the young man's calm and determination. They stayed quietly at a distance and waited.

Just as Nazar had hoped, the fighters, with their rumbling vehicles and their rifles waving in the air and their triumphant shouts of Allahu Akbar which sent shivers down his spine, passed down the street and were now out of sight.

Nazar breathed a deep sigh and returned to Amira and her father, "They are gone. It is safe for us to cross now." Then he paused to think a moment, "I have an idea. I think we could go from here to our family farmhouse and rest there, maybe stay there for the night. You will hear the roosters in the morning but otherwise it is quiet, and we will be outside of the town. I don't think anyone will notice us. We have chickens and there may be some bread and other food left over—if no one has broken into the house. Something tells me that Baba is not at home—I don't know where he is—but we will be safe there. At least we will have plenty of eggs to eat."

Yousif smiled and said, "You are very clever, Nazar. It may be a good idea—as long as it does not take us too far away from our plan. We want to be going towards the road that goes east to Erbil. You understand that, so we can get a ride."

Amira joined in, "How much time do you think it would take for us to get there? You know, Nazar, we cannot move too quickly as we are carrying my father."

"I think maybe an hour and a half—possibly two hours—so we could be there later in the afternoon but certainly long before it gets dark."

So that is exactly what they did. They gathered up their satchels and lifted up Amira's father once again, traveling in the direction of the farmhouse with Nazar as their guide.

They made their way outside of the deserted town, noticed only by one defiant old woman, who made it clear to them—by displaying a huge frown on her face—that she was not going to abandon her home. She appeared to be mentally challenged, completely oblivious to the danger she would be facing by staying behind. Yet Amira was impressed with her. She mentioned to Yousif that she saw in the woman's fiery eyes an unrelenting courage and determination. She was not going to let herself be intimidated by the evil warriors.

Other than this stubborn old woman, there was no one else to be seen, and no one to help them on their journey.

After about an hour or so of walking on a country road, Amira realised that they needed to refill their water containers. Once again, Nazar had a solution, "My cousin Ghadir lives not too far from here. His family has a well. Their water is sweet and clear. It is better than the water at our farm. I will show you the way to their property. They have dogs, but the dogs know me, so I am hoping they won't bark when they see us. I don't know if anyone is there now. Everyone in the area seems to be gone just as you say, Amira—but I know they would want us to stop and get water from their well."

"Maybe this will be our last stop before we arrive at your farmhouse?" said Amira, "You see—how the good Lord is giving us the strength to go on."

"Yes, I think it will be the last stop," said Nazar, "we are all holding up, and your father is peaceful."

Ghadir's home was a modest cinder block farmhouse with wheat fields surrounding it, and a few scattered farm animals. Only a small portion of the wheat had been harvested, and then the rest of it was left untouched, as if the farmer started the harvesting but then his work was abruptly interrupted.

When they arrived, two huge scraggly dogs came out of the barn and greeted Nazar, jumping up on him and licking his face. As they jumped on him and wagged their tails, Nazar petted them and gently called their names, "Good boys! Hello Sabou'ee. Hello Dyskey. Nice to see you. *Shloun el shabab el tayba? Zehneen?"* (Which means—How are you doing? Everything OK?) Then he turned to Amira and Yousif, "They are not always this way; it is a relief that they are peaceful. Most of the time they bark very loudly at strangers, even when they are quite a distance from the home! Maybe they could smell that it was me. You know, dogs can smell things pretty far away."

Just as Nazar had said, there was an old stone well with the sweetest and clearest water Amira and her father had ever tasted. They rested in the shade, filled up their containers, and planned the remaining stretch of the journey ahead.

Nazar then told Amira about the path which runs along the stream to his farmhouse, "I have good news for you, Amira. Towards the back of this property, there is a stream with a path alongside of it."

Amira listened, wondering what was next, "Yes?"

"And the stream will take us to our farmhouse, and there are no roads with cars that we will have to cross, and maybe no one will even see us. The stream water is not good for drinking, but if we get overheated, we can at least cool our feet and wash our faces with the stream right nearby us."

"But is the path wide enough to walk on? And we are carrying my father."

"Yes, it is very flat, and wide enough to be able to carry him. We have to watch here and there to make sure we don't trip on the roots. I know the stream well. I used to play in it all the time with my friends when I was younger. Also, I remember—there are a few date palm trees along the path that I might be able to climb up, and get some dates for us. It will be a good snack."

"I suppose you could try. That is a nice thought, if you can manage to climb with that wounded arm. Just remember: the most important thing is that we don't want to be seen, Nazar."

"I know—I know, but this will be the safest way for us to go. I am certain."

"Well you have been right so far, and this way we will hopefully arrive at your farmhouse before it gets dark."

"Amira, it will be well before dark, I am sure of that."

The three travellers retrieved all their supplies and their fresh water in jugs, and of course, they carried Amira's father, who seemed to be getting heavier and heavier as the journey went on. Nazar's arm was hurting him from time to time, but he tried to not show it on his face. Along the stream, in addition to the date palms, there were very tall Arabic gum trees scattered in different places to give them shade, and some willows rustling in the breeze. So Nazar's idea was not a bad one at all.

After about an hour, they stopped along the side of the stream. Amira washed her face and her father's face with some water, and they rested.

"Nazar," she said carefully, "maybe you should tell me more about what happened to you yesterday? You have been through a lot. Why didn't you get away with the crowds that were escaping from the village yesterday evening? It's OK if you don't want to talk about it—but it was so strange that you were all alone this morning when I saw you walking down the steps of the church."

"Well—yesterday morning I overheard my father and my brother Samir talking. Samir was told to help out at Uncle Basim's farm, and they left a note for me. When I came downstairs, they were gone. The note said I had to stay there and do all my chores and not go anywhere. It said—*wait till we get back.*

"So, I did all the chores. I fed the animals and cleaned my room. No one called. No one came by. I decided to run over to my friend Noori's house which isn't too far from our family's farm. I saw Noori and we kicked the soccer ball around. Noori's mother was not the same. She was upset and seemed very frightened. Noori's father was packing up their family vehicle as if they were getting ready for a family trip. But it could not have been a vacation as he was not in a happy mood. She said there could be a danger from mortars and explosions and bullets in our area, and that they were going to try to 'evacuate or seek shelter'—those were her words. When I heard them talking about bullets, that really scared me. I didn't know what evacuate meant so she told me they thought it was best to get away. I told her I needed to wait for Baba and Samir to come back. They tried calling my father but there was no way to reach him. Maybe his phone was not working? Noori was also getting very upset and frightened.

"He said, 'Nazar, you must come with us, you cannot wait for your father.' I told them that maybe I could try to reach Samir, my elder brother, and he could pick me up at home and take me away. But Samir did not answer either. I did not understand what was going on.

"Noori's father was putting a lot of stuff in their car—there was food, backpacks, a computer, suitcases, and even a photo album…They said they would be preparing to leave in early evening along with many of their friends and relatives. So, they gave me a quick lunch with Noori, then I said goodbye to them all. I said I would stop by later on if Samir and Baba did not show up.

"Soon after that, I heard explosions in the distance, almost like the loud thunder we hear with our violent summer storms. I even stepped outside to look for lightning, but there was nothing. My mind tried so hard to avoid the reality that the explosions were getting closer to me. The noises were getting louder and louder. I was really worried. Amira, there were no signs of any storm in the air. The trees and the fields were still, and the sky was completely blue. Not a cloud. Then I suddenly felt like someone punched me in the stomach when I finally admitted the truth to myself—*this was no storm. These were the rumblings of war!*

"The sun was starting to go down. I thought I needed to do something. I could not wait any longer. So, I went out on the road and hitched a ride to get as close as possible to Uncle Basim's farm, then I ran the rest of the way."

Here Nazar suddenly became quiet. Incredibly strong emotions were pouring into his young face. He waved his arms in the air as if waving his arms would make it easier for the words to come out of his mouth, "I saw Samir and he looked at me. He was so angry to see me. It cut like a knife. Then Uncle Basim and Samir made me get out of there right away and go back home. Uncle Basim gave me his old motorbike and I started down the road. Then, when I looked back—I saw—I saw," he swallowed hard. He could not speak any longer. He took a deep breath,

"Amira—I saw the two explosions right there at the farmhouse. Both their vehicles were hit by a huge tank. There was heavy black smoke and dust flying into the air, and huge flaming fires everywhere. There was the stench of burning rubber filling the air. Then the roof of uncle's farmhouse caught on fire. I called out for my brother. Samir! Samir! I called out for Uncle Basim. But they did not answer. They were gone, Amira. They were gone in an instant."

Amira wrapped her arms around Nazar. She said nothing, only holding him tightly while the tears poured from his eyes onto her shoulder like a waterfall. She felt his heart pounding, and gently rubbed his back to ease his sorrow.

Amira's father listened to everything Nazar had said while he sat gazing at the stream. Nazar sat down on a large rock next to him, holding his head in his hands. He was so shaken that he completely forgot to tell Amira the rest of the story about how he sped back to Karemlesh on his bike (ignoring his brother's command to go home), how he ran out of gas and had to sprint the rest of the way; about his visit with Aram in the butcher shop, how he saw the villagers fleeing with their belongings, and finally, how he had witnessed the total desecration of Mar Addai that very morning. Amira was wise enough to not ask any more questions.

Then Yousif looked at Nazar with his kind eyes and got his attention, "This is a great suffering which you are facing,

Nazar, and at such a young age. I understand what you are feeling. You have witnessed the killing of your beloved brother Samir and your Uncle Basim. You are probably thinking every moment about your father. Will you see him again? Will he be safe? Where has he gone? We have lived through so much sorrow in our land now. So many thousands who have lost fathers or mothers or brothers or sisters, so many badly hurt or wounded, so many homes and shops abandoned—so much destruction—everywhere.

"Let us not lose hope, even if we don't understand where the good Lord is leading us, or what the future may bring. I trust He will not abandon you, Nazar. Let me tell you something. I believe your father is not harmed and that he is looking for you as we speak. Yesterday he most likely helped the elderly reach safety, and now he must be trying to find you. Don't ask me why I believe this, but something deep inside me tells me it is true.

"And I trust the good Lord will not abandon our people. Let us continue to hope and to persevere. I believe He will bring good out of the evil which has come upon us. Look, Nazar, He has sent you to us. It is as if He has sent us an angel to guide us on our journey. He will bring us to safety. I have not given up my trust in Him."

Nazar splashed his hands in the water, continuing to weep. He sat in silence. He wanted with all his being to say a prayer. He wanted to ask God to help him find his father, or to bring his father to him, but he had no words. Only a loud and distressed sigh emerged from his lips.

He suddenly heard the beautiful singing of the Skylark. It was an exquisite melody, heavenly, piercing the depths of his soul. As the Skylark continued to sing his melody, Nazar experienced an indescribable peace and consolation pour over him. He was imbued with an inexplainable hope that his wordless prayer had been answered. He sat completely still for a few moments, resting in this unexpected moment of peace. Then he washed the dust and tears off his face and took a deep breath, "I think we should go on now."

And so, they continued along the path that Nazar promised would lead to his farmhouse. The afternoon sun was getting warmer, but an occasional tree along the route provided the shade they needed. The Skylark was following closely behind them, occasionally stirring them onward with his celestial melodies.

Evening at Baba's Farmhouse

As Nazar had said, towards the end of the afternoon, and well before dark, they arrived at his family's farmhouse. The house was a sturdy old stone structure, not too big and not too small. There was a peace surrounding the property and everything was in its place, exactly as Nazar had left it the day before.

"The house is untouched," said Amira, "The good Lord has been merciful to us."

Nazar said, "I know where the key is hidden. I can let us in. Then I will go into the barn and see if I can get us some eggs."

"Don't worry about the eggs now, Nazar. You need to rest. We all should rest."

"Yes, I will rest, but I want to make sure there is something we can have for dinner, and I need to check the animals in the barn to see that they are all fed. I know they were not fed since I was here yesterday."

They entered the home which had a small kitchen table with four chairs, and two bedrooms, one used by Baba and one for Nazar and Samir. Nazar again felt like he was being suddenly punched in the stomach, thinking that he had lost his brother and might never see his father again, that he would have to flee from this beautiful home filled with so many memories. Tears came to his eyes for a few moments, but he ignored them with a maturity beyond his age, and once again he focused on what had to be done to help his fellow travellers.

Nazar suggested to Amira that she rest in Baba's bedroom while her father and he take the two beds in the boys' room. Everything was simple, neat and clean, and the feeling of peace which was present outdoors also visited the home. There was a gentle breeze permeating the house when Nazar opened the windows. Yousif could feel the gentle wind cooling his forehead and stirring the curtains. He could sense the peace in the room, but he knew it was not from the breeze. The birds were singing their late afternoon melodies. The Skylark was perched in the tree right above the home. He was not noticed.

Nazar went over to Yousif and sat on the edge of the old man's bed. He looked at Nazar with a serene expression, "What is it, Nazar? I see you are very sad. You should be sad, since your own eyes have witnessed such tragedies. You have a question?" he said, looking at the young man's lonely, distressed face.

"Sir—would it be all right if—I called you *Amo Yousif?*" (He used the Sureth word *Amo*, which is an affectionate name for an uncle or a beloved relative) "I feel like you are a new friend for me. More than that, I feel like I am part of your family now, and that you really care about what happens to me."

"Of course, you can call me *Amo Yousif*. I would like that very much. As long as I am on this earth, I will be your Amo. I will be here for you. Don't be troubled. All will be well, Nazar!" and he smiled at the boy. Then he drifted off to sleep.

Nazar looked at the calm face of Amira's father and couldn't quite figure out how he could be so free of agitation, given all he had been through in the last few days. He laid down on the other bed for a few minutes, tossing and turning, but he was not able to rest. His eye caught various clothing items in his bedroom closet, and he noticed his brother Samir's t-shirts and jerseys with team numbers and all the bright slogans on them. A beautiful memory came to his mind of all the nature activities they had done together over the years of growing up—climbing rocks, forging streams, lighting fires, and camping out—and more tears came to his eyes. His injured arm began to throb with pain. Then the traumatic memories of the explosions at his uncle's farm invaded his mind with a great cloud of darkness. He heard the tense voice of Samir calling his name when he arrived there. He heard his own troubled voice crying out—Samir! Uncle Basim! and then the deadly silence.

He was determined to break the spell of the memories before they crippled him. He peeked in the other bedroom and noticed Amira was snoring gently. Then he resolved to do a few chores while things were quiet, as he was most concerned about feeding the farm animals in the barn and fetching eggs from the chickens. He thought the eggs would be the easiest dinner to cook up for his guests, and it was something he was very good at—making omelettes with new farm greens and the local cheese. There was some fresh milk ready to drink, and some water from the well. *But,* Nazar thought, *they will notice that our well water is not as good as Ghadir's…still it is water, and they are thirsty.*

When Amira and her father woke up from their naps, it was almost dark. Amira walked into the kitchen. Nazar was at the stove making the omelettes.

"Hello, Amira, I have dinner almost ready. Doesn't it smell wonderful? And I found some old crusty bread and I am warming it in the oven so it will be a little softer. And we have some milk, and here is the water from our well. At least for tonight we won't be hungry, and when we wake up in the morning, we will have some food inside of us. So, we can finish our journey."

"Nazar, you have even set the table for us. And where did these flowers come from?" Nazar had put a few wildflowers in a vase on the table. The setting was so pleasant, it could have been in a Cezanne painting, "I must help my father to come to the table, so he can join us for this surprise feast. If you stay on one side of him, I will get on the other, and we can help him to the table."

The evening passed quickly as they ate like ravenous wolves while Amira's father entertained them with stories of his work as a mason, building all kinds of homes and shops for his customers in the village. Then he recalled humorous stories about Amira when she was a little girl, always getting into fights with the boys next door. "Do you remember Jonas, next door?" he said to his daughter, "Remember the picnic we were having in the back of the farmhouse, and you were so proud of your slice of bread with that big piece of lamb on top—and Jonas looked over the wall, took his slingshot and knocked the meat right off your bread with his little pebble. He had a good aim, didn't he?" They all laughed. "Glad that pebble didn't hit your face—your face has always been beautiful, Amira, it has never changed all these years, your goodness shines through your lovely hazel eyes. And your inner beauty is even more stunning than the beauty of your face."

Nazar suddenly became very energised, "You know, Amo Yousif, I am also very good with the sling shot. I sometimes bring it to the church festival. I hide it in my pocket—so Baba doesn't see it. I can knock anything off a piece of pita bread-lamb, chicken, you name it—and from quite a distance away. It is lots of fun. You should see their faces when their big piece of chicken suddenly flies into the air!"

Amira was surprised, holding back her smile, "Nazar, I am shocked—I see that you have a mischievous side to your personality."

"Well, Amira, I am good most of the time." replied Nazar proudly.

Then, almost as if no sadness had ever crossed their path, Yousif surprised them with another touch of humour, "I want you all to know that in a few days it will be my birthday, and I want to celebrate this evening, as I am with such special people. Is that OK?"

Amira and Nazar nodded.

"So, we are going to have my favourite food tonight. OK?"

"It's OK with us." replied Amira and Nazar.

"Amira knows what it is…we are going to have a *samak mazgoof*."

"Samak mazgoof?" replied Nazar, with surprise, "Amo Yousif, we don't have any samak here and we can't go out to catch it now. And besides, I don't think we have the spices that we need to cook the mazgoof."

Amira smiled, "Well, Nazar, samak mazgoof is my father's favourite food, and he wants to celebrate his birthday tonight. He prefers the mazgoof preparation with a fish, rather than with chicken or beef. In fact, his favourite is when I go to the market and buy him a big—rather ugly—river carp. And when I prepare it for him, not often I can assure you, I bring out the entire cooked fish and put it on a platter right in front of him. I like it too, but he eats most of it. It is not pretty to look at, but we both find it tasty. After I grill it, I make a special sauce with spices and pour it on top of the fish."

Then Nazar understood the game, "Oh yes, Amira. I am surprised Amo did not prefer the *rafish*, our Euphrates softshell turtle. Nothing is more delicious than that. But he chose the samak, oh well, so please bring out the—the—mazgoof right away. And don't let it get cold! I would like to eat the eyes, is that OK? They are crunchy and delicious." He made everyone laugh.

Yousif pretended to be very serious for a brief moment. "You know, Nazar, you are not quite right about those crunchy eyes. When Amira makes samak mazgoof for me, the eyes are always soft and squishy, just the way I like them."

Amira smiled as she looked at her father.

Then Nazar put the last forkful of omelette in his mouth, continuing on with the game almost as if he didn't hear Yousif's comment. "Oh yes, this is the best fish I have ever had, and the eyes and that ugly head—they are wonderful—unforgettable, don't you think? And eating those eyes is good for my vision! I don't want to be wearing any eyeglasses when I go on to the university. Amira, your sauce has amazing flavour, although it needs more salt. I hope you are pleased, Amo Yousif? I caught the mazgoof myself in the Tigris. Or was it the Euphrates? I can't remember. I must confess—there were a few old slimy tires I caught before I finally snagged that samak!"

Amira was happily engaged in the fantasy. She winked at Nazar, "And what about the broom you snagged?"

Nazar was caught off guard, "Broom?" he paused, then his mind went to work, "Ah yes, Amira, *that* broom. You know it was quite ancient. Maybe 1600 BC. It was stuck underneath some barnacled stones from the ruins of Babylon when I caught it on my hook. I gave it to Amira so she could sweep the house."

Everyone was laughing so hard that Yousif was shedding tears. He forced himself to stop so he could catch his breath.

"Well, I am enjoying this dish immensely." he pretended, as he also nibbled on his last forkful of omelette, which had gotten cold by then, "This is the best samak mazgoof I have ever tasted. This is my best birthday party ever. Did you know, Nazar, that on this very farmland in the Nineveh plains of Iraq, quite a long time ago—well before you were born, Alexander the Great was charging by on horseback with his vast armies. He was chasing after King Darius and the Persians. Alexander chased his enemies across Nineveh all the way to Arbela. You've heard of Arbela, haven't you, Nazar? These days we call it Erbil. And now, on our table, right here in front of us, all I can see leftover are these big fish bones! Here, in this same historic location—where Alexander the Great conquered the Persians, the three of us have conquered the mazgoof!"

Then Amira looked at her watch. The mood in the kitchen suddenly got serious. She worked out a plan with Yousif and Nazar. They would get to bed early and rise with the dawn. Nazar assured her that the two roosters are always very loud right at dawn, so they would not need an alarm clock. Nazar agreed to take care of any chores with the animals as soon as he woke up. He would get more water from the well to fill their containers, and Amira said she would gather whatever food she could put in their backpacks for the journey. Then they would lock up everything and walk along the small winding gravel road that passed in front of the house until it reached the main road to Erbil.

Before going to bed, Nazar looked at Amira with a smile, as if he was not done with telling jokes, "Amira, tomorrow is the day we will need the Good Samaritan to show up on the road to take us to Erbil. I hope he doesn't have a tiny Toyota Yaris."

Amira laughed, "But we won't need a giant moving van either, will we? I will ask the good Lord for a pickup truck."

Then she hugged the young man, a remarkable young man who had demonstrated such great courage and steadfastness, "You are amazing, Nazar. We could not have done any of this without you. And we are almost at the finish line! Now let us get a good night's sleep."

Nazar replied, "Yes, I am going to get to bed—but first, I want to step outside the house for just a few minutes and look at the stars. Baba and I used to do that a lot, and I think tonight may not be perfect, but it should be clear enough. I think I might even see a shooting star."

Amira said, "Well, now that my father is in bed, I might like to join you if I could."

"Come with me," said Nazar, "we will go outside—away from the lights of the house and step into the wheat fields, then look up. This time of year, the stars are amazing. And you know that the moon is not out yet, so we will see the stars even more clearly. You can't see them that way from the centre of the village."

Amira went out with Nazar into the wheat fields. There was a soothing summer evening breeze passing through the wheat fields and stirring the harvest. The crickets and other night creatures were making pleasant melodies. They looked up at the sky. Amira was stunned by the glittering lights. Nazar almost felt like he could reach up and touch them and bring them to earth. When they began to talk, the Skylark woke up from his deep sleep and listened to their conversation.

"Amira?"

"Yes, Nazar."

"You talk about the good Lord, *Le bon Dieu*."

"Yes, that's right."

"But, Amira, do you really believe that God is good? Now that we see all the terrible things that have happened to us. You were forced to leave your home. You may not ever go back again. And my brother Samir, and Uncle Basim—and Baba. I don't know what happened to him. Maybe he is gone. Maybe I will never see him again."

Amira's eyes remained fixed on the heavens.

"Nazar, would a *Tashya Alousa* create such beauty?"

Amira was using the Chaldean words for *cruel tyrant*.

Nazar paused. He could not answer.

Then Amira put her arm on his shoulder, "Yes, Nazar, the suffering is real. But the goodness is inescapable. It is surrounding us.

"You know, Nazar, my grandfather, and then my father, treasured a favourite Bible that they used to read from each evening after dinner. They read to the family. Of course, the Bible was in Sureth. We all cherished that moment. We sat quietly and listened to every word. They loved to read from the psalms and sometimes they got us to memorise the verses. There is one verse that comes to mind tonight. I have never forgotten it." Out of the depths of her heart, she recited the verse from Psalm 91 to Nazar in Sureth:

Bet Paree bet Kaselokh, Okhoth Golpanee B Arqet
La gzadet min zdotha det lelee.

Which means—

He will conceal you in His wings.
You will not fear the terror of the night.

"Yes, we are concealed in His wings, Nazar, whatever the suffering, however painful, we are not forgotten. He is with us.

"You know, it broke my heart, but I had to leave that Bible behind. It was too heavy to carry. As you have seen with your own eyes, we had to leave everything behind. Maybe one day we will return to our home, and the first thing I promise to do when I enter the doorway is to look for that Bible. I will find the page with those special verses from that psalm, and I will fall on my knees and thank the good Lord for His mercy to us."

Then she hugged Nazar and they paused in silence, looking at the magnificent stars. Nazar wondered how she could have such faith.

A brilliant shooting star sped across the sky. And they went inside.

Nazar and Amira went to bed, wondering about the next day, whether it would be yet another fearful day of darkness, or a day of sunshine and hope. Yousif was fast asleep, not troubled or worried, deeply at peace.

"…in the wilderness…you saw how the Lord your God carried you, just as one carries a child, all the way that you travelled until you reached this place."
—Deuteronomy 1:31

The Good Samaritan

At dawn, as predicted, the two roosters began to crow so loudly that it was impossible to ignore them. Amira was tossing a bit in bed when it was still mostly dark outside. She checked her watch as soon as she heard their ruckus. The two other travellers woke up soon after her as the sun was rising and as the birds were singing their morning lauds. Amira thought, *Thank the good Lord for this lovely bird song. At least I am not listening to the sounds of war and more deadly explosions. All is quiet.*

The Skylark too was there. He was peeking inside Nazar's bedroom window and tapping on it, as if to show he was concerned that he wakeup on time for the journey ahead.

They ate a simple breakfast of bread and milk, then packed everything up according to plan, and started out on the gravel road which passed in front of the farmhouse.

Nazar guided them. His shoulder and arm were beginning to throb again with pain. He still managed to help carry Yousif, the water, and his backpack, "If we continue to walk on this gravel road for another half hour or so, we should arrive at the big road that goes to Erbil in the east and Mosul in the west."

Time passed quickly. No one saw the three of them on their journey that morning. The heavy morning fog lingered throughout the plains. Everything was quiet when they reached the black asphalt, two lane highway, that would lead them to shelter. They went to the side of the road in the direction of Erbil. Yousif cautioned them that they might be wise to hide nearby the road just in case the warrior men drove by. But Amira said to him that they would have to take the risk. If someone quickly drove by who could help them and they were not able to be seen, they would lose their opportunity.

They waited along the side of the road, sipping their water. Nazar was starting to feel very warm and a bit dizzy. Amira put her hand on his forehead and noticed he had a fever, "I think there must be an infection with that cut on your arm. It is not surprising. Look at how busy you have been, with no time to rest. If we can just get you to the clinic where my sister Zara is, she will take care of you. You will be able to get some medicine and I am sure she will make you better, Nazar."

In the distance they heard what sounded like a large truck approaching. The morning fog made it impossible to see what kind of truck it was. It was making a great deal of creaking and banging noises, which got louder and louder, and seemed to be spewing out smoke from the engine, which mixed with the fog surrounding it. Nazar continued to stare at what seemed to be a large black vehicle. The fog and his increasing dizziness made it impossible to determine if it was one of the enemy trucks. But, as it got closer, they could see there were no men on top of the truck waving their rifles. There were no shouts of Allahu Akbar. Amira could see at last that it was a pickup truck! The back of the truck was piled high with bags and boxes and random furniture. Still, the closer it got, the truck was sounding more and more scary with those strange noises, and the driver—was he wearing a turban on his head? They could not see the face of the driver—who was he? Was he a friend or an enemy?

Amira mumbled a prayer with a strong feeling of apprehension in her stomach, "Jesus, Mary and Joseph, please protect us."

The pickup truck stopped and a tanned muscular young man with a white turban on his head abruptly got out and ran towards them. He looked at the three travellers with a steady stare, then gazed at Amira's father lying on his stretcher on the road, knelt down, squinted and looked at his face.

"Yousif! Are you hurt? What happened?" he called out in Arabic in a tone of alarm.

Yousif looked up at the man, replying in Sureth, "Omar! Is it really you? Omar, I can't believe my eyes. Amira—this is unbelievable—Omar is one of the new young builders from my company. He is my best worker. He gets all the masons hired and he trains them. He has become almost like a son to me."

"OK Father, yes, I think I remember you telling me about him. This is very good news. I will ask him now to help us."

Before she could say a word, Omar interrupted, very agitated, "My Sureth is not at all good…let me try my best to explain. I went back to Karemlesh to gather some things from my house. It was maybe stupid for me to do, too risky, but I did it, and now—would you mind if I speak in Arabic? It will be easier for me." So, after Amira nodded, he continued in Arabic, "Thank you. I am on the way to Erbil to meet up with my wife and children who are there. I don't know if I will ever see our home again. You must come with me. You cannot stay here on the road. Not too far back I think I saw an enemy truck. Really not sure with the fog this morning. He probably won't be following us to Erbil, but, trust me, you don't want to be found here—by them!"

Amira replied in Arabic, thinking quickly. Fortunately, she was fluent in Omar's language, "I think we might be able to make room for my father in the back of the truck...I must say you do have a lot of furniture and boxes...but I think there could be room there, and Nazar—" she paused, looking around for Nazar, and suddenly noticed in shock that he had collapsed on the pavement in exhaustion, "Nazar is not well. He may have fainted. Maybe worse. He will need medical care very soon. Let us put him in the back with my father on that old mattress, so he can just rest and be still until we arrive at the clinic."

"What clinic?" said Omar.

"The Holy Family clinic in the historic Christian enclave of Ankawa. Perhaps you have not heard of Ankawa? It is one of the districts in the city of Erbil. I can help you with the directions once we get closer to the city. My sister Zara runs the clinic. They call her Sister Caterina. I am sure the sisters will be able to help Nazar, and maybe also get my father back on his feet again."

"Oh, now I understand why you were waiting on the road. I didn't know Yousif had been injured. Maybe at work? After I went home the other day? Yes, I will take you there immediately, as long as my truck holds up. I think I have just enough gas—with maybe a thimble—full extra."

So they moved some boxes around and carefully positioned Nazar and Yousif into the back of the pickup truck, and Amira got into the passenger seat in the front alongside Omar, after removing several more bags and boxes from that seat before she could squeeze herself in there. Then the truck sputtered along on the road to Erbil.

"This will take possibly a few hours or so as long as we don't run into any danger from enemy fighters," said Omar, "I see you are comfortable speaking in Arabic, so if we can keep talking in Arabic that will be easier for me—just so we understand each other. I really must warn you now. We will see some ugly things along the way. Soon we are going to see the mobs of villagers heading to Erbil. They are escaping your village and many other villages of the Nineveh Plains. Thousands have already fled from the city of Mosul. Many of them are walking. Some will not survive the heat as it could be 120 degrees today. Some are very old. Some will get sick and die. Perhaps even children. Very sad. Some of the refugees have vehicles, but I hear they are having a tough time getting them into Erbil. We will be waiting a very long time at the checkpoint where the Peshmerga army is stationed. They want to make sure we are not carrying explosives. They don't want any suspicious vehicles getting into Erbil. So, I promise you, this is not going to be a comfortable, care-free drive in the countryside, if you know what I mean.

"I must apologise for my truck. I use it for everything, Amira—that is your name, am I right? I use it for my family and for work, it was old when I bought it, and we are always transporting heavy stones and equipment back and forth to the work sites, and," here he chuckled a little bit, "you know, your father had been pestering me to get rid of the truck and replace it with something less—'frightening' was the word he used, and he told me to drive it off a cliff and I said to him, 'There are no cliffs in the Nineveh Plains, Yousif.' We laughed. So, he said, 'Well, then drive it into the river and forget about it.' I said to him, 'Which river? The Tigris or the Euphrates—or perhaps the Great Zab?' Can you believe we were laughing just the other day about it, Amira? As you can see, I had no time to start looking for a replacement. And not a lot of money. We are not a wealthy family. I'm sure you can guess that we live in the poorest part of the village. We are just getting by.

"So, Amira, you are living with your father. You have the privilege of seeing him all the time. He is a wonderful man. A blessing to work with. Kind, charitable, and very capable. I know he has said very complimentary things about you. Pardon me if this is too personal a question, but is your husband not well enough to help you? This is an almost impossible situation that you and that young man have taken on."

Amira replied with a tone of melancholy, "I have no husband now. Over twenty years ago I married a wonderful man. His name was Fady. He was an engineer, very well positioned with his career. We had been friends for years, then we fell in love. I was crazy about him but I was patient. I waited for him to finish his studies before we got married. We were going to buy a house and start our family. He was an advisor for many of the oil wells in Kuwait, so he used to travel there a lot. Omar, I still find this very emotional, pardon me. He lost his life…when the oil wells were torched by—by that infamous, and now deceased dictator—our *Trona*—thank

God he is gone. I will not honour his name by bringing it to my lips."

Amira had been conversing with Omar in fluent Arabic throughout their entire ride in his pickup truck. But, in an unexpected burst of anger, she uttered the Sureth word *Trona* to voice her disdain for the tyrant.

"It was a horrific time, Omar. You might be too young to remember any of the events that happened then. You are indeed fortunate if you know nothing about it. Many of the engineers and construction workers lost their lives. It was so dangerous to be working there when the wells were torched. My life was burdened with deep sadness for many years after that. Then, miraculously perhaps, over time the sadness lifted, thanks to the good Lord. But I did not marry again."

A tear came to Omar's eye, "I am very sorry to hear about your husband. I was too young then to know that I was living in such a horrific time for our country. As I grew up, I lived through other nightmares that suffocated our land, perhaps worse than the thick dark poisonous smoke that poured out from those oil wells for so many months.

"You know, Amira, the way I see things, all these wars over the years, have impoverished our country and deeply scarred each one of us. The loss of one life—think of it—your husband was killed, and his death brought you unspeakable suffering and loss. Then, you did not raise a family as you had dreamed, so each of those children you hoped to raise never came into this world; maybe one would have been a talented musician; maybe another one, a doctor, curing all kinds of illnesses; maybe another a great builder like Yousif; maybe another, a future mother of some well-cared-for grandchildren. So, as I see it, we are all impoverished because these wonderful lives never came to be...These wars, Amira," Omar sighed, "...look what these terrible wars have done to us."

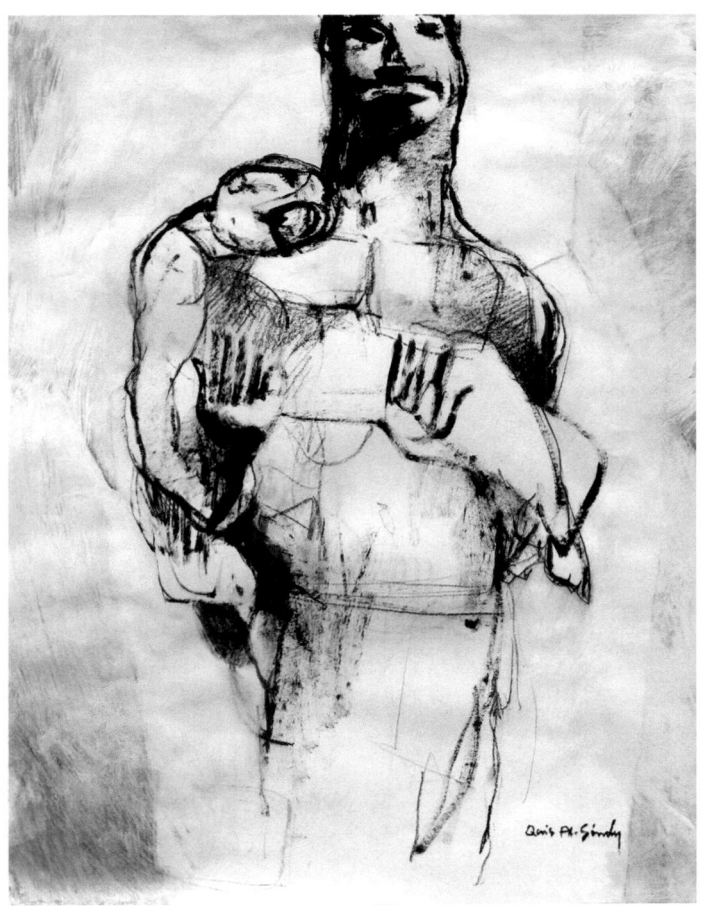

Then Amira changed the subject, and with it, her mood changed as well, "But Omar, pardon me for asking, why is your family leaving Karemlesh? You are not a Christian family—you are followers of Islam—am I right? So, you would not be tormented by the militants. I don't think they would harm you."

He replied with a tone of sadness mixed with anger, "Our town has been destroyed. Our friends have been forced to leave. How can I do business here and raise my family? There are many sincere followers of Islam in this area who have also become their targets. So, we fled from the town with many of our Christian neighbours just the other evening. It was a terrible night, so sad, so many tears, so many crying children. No, Amira, there is no place for us any longer in Karemlesh. Our life there is over.

"And like a fool I decided to come back to take some things from our home, our family treasures. Maybe they aren't treasures after all. Why am I risking my life for this stuff? Who knows what we will be able to do with it when I get to Erbil? If you could see the thousands of refugees who are crowded there now, it is so sad. There is barely enough space for the people—no room for our belongings.

"You know, now that I think about it, Amira—Allah must be looking out for you. Of course—you Christians say—the Lord. We both give thanks to Him for the goodness He showers upon us each day."

"Yes, I say *the good Lord*. I say that all the time, Omar."

"If I did not go back to my house, you would have had no truck to take you to Erbil. The roads are empty heading west, and there is no one coming from that direction anymore. You will soon see a massive migration of people fleeing everywhere in the Nineveh Plains and heading east to Erbil. There are countless thousands ahead of us on this same road. You would have been in big trouble if my truck had not stopped for you."

"Well," replied Amira with a slight smile on her face, "you know, it was only last night I said to Nazar that a pickup truck would be just right. And here it is—I admit, it is no golden chariot, but I think it will get us where we need to go."

Amira changed the subject once again when a new question came to her mind, "Omar, I was wondering, if you don't mind my asking, you seem to be an intelligent and thoughtful young man. You never wanted to go on to the university? You would have been a great teacher."

Omar replied with a touch of regret, "Truthfully, I was a very good student, Amira, and I was encouraged to advance to the university. I love history, and I loved reading, and I still read a lot and keep current with the world's troubles. But, you understand, I come from a poor family. When I was a kid, my father was disabled and unable to work, and he died when I was a teenager. My mother desperately needed me to work and bring in money for the family. I'm sure you've heard this story before. At first, I went abroad to make money in construction. I'd routinely wire the money to my mother. Then, after I thought the war was over and the regime had been toppled, I came back to Nineveh, and started to work with your father. Life is full of many twists and turns, don't you think? I was wrong about the war being over. Never a moment of peace in this country. So here we are today, escaping to Erbil."

Amira suddenly recalled a memory, and a smile came to her face, "You know, Omar, your remarks about life being full of twists and turns reminds me of one of the students I taught years ago. He used to say to me—" interrupting her sentence, she then began to speak in a heavily accented English, 'Life is full of curve balls.'

"Curve balls?" replied Omar, struggling tremendously to pronounce the English words.

"Yes, it is a baseball term," said Amira with a gentle laugh.

"I don't play baseball, Amira. I never played baseball. And I don't care too much for Americans, to be honest. They have too much stuff."

"A bit like you? With all your stuff?" Amira teased. Omar laughed.

"Please go on, Amira."

"I wish I could remember that boy's name. He was absolutely crazy about baseball. His family had one of those satellite dishes so I suppose they watched sports on TV all the time. Anyway, he was the one who told me what a curve ball is. He never stopped talking about baseball...so I learned a lot about that game, although I never watched it. And he said that life is full of *curve balls*. He could even fake an American accent."

"Sorry, I am not following you..." said Omar, not sure of where she was going with her remarks.

"Well, when a pitcher throws a curve ball, he makes it almost impossible for the batter to hit the ball. So, you understand? Life throws many curve balls at us."

"Well," said Omar, pretending to be disgruntled, "your saying, Amira, is of no use to me. Those English words 'curve ball' are impossible for me to pronounce. I will never remember them! The English language—how can anyone speak it? It is impossible!" Then, he burst out laughing.

Checkpoint in the Wilderness

The time on the road passed quickly, with Omar and Amira bantering back and forth in Arabic, trying hard to distract each other from the distress of their situation. As they looked out the windows, the morning fog was gradually being burned off by the merciless August sun. To keep their gas use as low as possible, they didn't put on air conditioning and opened their windows. The air from the fields was still refreshing. They saw the abundant wheat fields of the plains sparkling in the daylight, ready for harvest, but there was no trace of farmworkers or other villagers outside doing their routine chores.

Other than the beauty of the vast blue sky and the wheat fields, they witnessed more and more hardship and tragedy as they stared out the windows. As Omar had predicted, they saw endless groupings of people from various towns, many of whom were elderly, resting beside the road, trying to regain their strength to continue on to Erbil, which was still miles away. On the sides of the road, there was an infinite line of people of all ages walking with their satchels and belongings, hunched over, sweating, exhausted, but still slowly trudging ahead.

Omar observed, "These people started escaping from their villages well before yesterday. I am sure of that. They have been walking in this heat all this time. Can you imagine? Some of them slept along the side of the road during the night, and, as you know, Amira, it is cold at night, so I think a good deal of them must be sick by now. They are the ones without cars, or, who in haste or desperation, just left their vehicles behind, along with, Allah knows, what else they couldn't bring with them. They need water and food, but there are no emergency workers to help them out here on the plains."

Amira looked out at all the tired and wrinkled faces with compassion, wishing she could do something, anything, to relieve their suffering, "Omar, I feel so frustrated that we cannot take them along with us in our truck. Where are all the vehicles?"

"They are all in front of us—thousands of them. Soon we will need to slow down to a crawl as the line of cars and trucks backs up. We'll have to endure several miles of delay in the blazing sun—right before the checkpoint. We will also see larger and larger crowds of people walking, and they will need to get through the checkpoint as well."

"I don't remember any checkpoint?"

"The Peshmerga soldiers have all moved east, closer to Erbil. They abandoned the Nineveh Plains which, you remember I'm sure, they had promised to protect. After the fall of Mosul, they rapidly retreated, leaving us all exposed to the unrelenting wrath of the militants. The Kurdish army is stationed outside Erbil now, and they are the ones who set up the checkpoint there. Unfortunately, they are no longer anywhere near here. We are on our own. Karemlesh is only one of many villages that were left as sitting ducks, as they say. And then you know what happened next? Word travelled quickly; thanks be to Allah. The Christians and everyone else in danger in these villages—including families with children just like ours—heard about the Peshmerga retreating. We decided we had no choice but to evacuate.

"I predict that in another day, or maybe two, as the villages in the Nineveh Plains become desolate, there will be well over one hundred thousand Christians arriving as refugees in Erbil. Then you know, of course, there are the Yazidis, the Shebak Muslims, and the rest of the Shia Muslims like our family. We are all headed into Erbil. There is no other place to go. Our number is even larger, some say maybe four hundred thousand or more non-Christians who are fleeing. Can you imagine, Amira? Over five hundred thousand people escaping Nineveh, and all of them converging on that small city! I wonder whether in recent years our planet has seen such a large concentration of displaced people—all amassed in this one location on the face of the earth. The four of us in this truck—we will be just a drop in the ocean of misery that will flood Erbil."

Amira was stunned, "It seems we Christians are always the ones caught in the middle of all the chaos—even though we were not the ones to cause it."

Omar replied in a tone absent of any emotion, "It is hard to know who the enemy hates more—the Christians—or everyone else."

Amira was thinking, not quite sure what to believe, "How do you know all this? How do you know about all these thousands of displaced people, Omar?"

"Well, you will recall, I was already in Erbil helping get my wife and family settled, before I made the stupid decision to come back to Nineveh to get our stuff."

"Yes, the stupid decision that saved our lives."

"That's right, Amira, I must try to see it through a providential lens, the way you do. So, when I was in Erbil, I talked with one of the aid workers standing next to a UN vehicle. There are a few UN vehicles here and there. I didn't see any Red Crescent trucks at all. And there were a few aid stations, which I guess other organisations had hastily set up—that's my impression. And I saw some volunteers. It is obvious to me that right now they are badly understaffed. There are long lines waiting for help at the different churches. They are running out of food and supplies. The guy from the UN was in panic mode, waving his hands and venting to me about the deluge of refugees they are already trying to care for, and the numbers they anticipate will be showing up in a matter of days."

Just as Omar had predicted, they began to witness tragic scenes along the roadside as they drove closer to their destination. They tried not to look. Still, there were too many of these episodes to shield from their field of vision. The most heart wrenching scenes were those of family members in small groupings rapidly reciting prayers for a loved one they had abruptly buried. As she looked out the window, Amira quietly prayed for the grieving as well as the souls of the deceased. There was nothing else she could do.

They both had the impression that the travellers buried their dead close to the road simply to save time. Some sites were marked with a makeshift cross, some with nothing on them. Many seemed to be buried very close to the surface, as if there were no tools available to the refugees to dig a deeper trench, or perhaps no time to do it with the urgency of escaping Nineveh.

They observed groupings of mourners of various religious backgrounds encircling bodies of older people who were placed flat on the ground while prayers were being said. They didn't have even a formal cloth to cover the dead. Omar slowed down the truck as they looked in shock at the tear-soaked face of a young mother, holding what must have been the dead body of her infant in her arms. She was wailing profusely. After all the prayers were completed, she appeared to refuse to place her baby in the makeshift grave.

Mixing with the vehicle fumes and the now stifling summer air, there was another smell which occasionally wafted into the open windows of the truck.

Amira was particularly sensitive to the odours, "Omar, what is it that we are smelling? It is terrible."

"It could be the stench of death, Amira. All it takes is two or three days after a man dies…some of these bodies must have been buried more than three days ago, perhaps the people fleeing from Mosul. And you see how a lot of these graves are very shallow, just a covering of dirt in some cases, plus, with this intense summer heat during the daytime."

Amira stopped him in mid-sentence, "Omar, please say no more. I suppose you are right—but this is unspeakably sad—my heart is broken." Omar and Amira were silent for several minutes, each trying to say some quiet prayers begging eternal peace for these unsuccessful victims of the exodus.

"Look there," said Omar, breaking the silence, "you see what I mean." He was pointing to another shallow grave to their right, with a rigid forearm jutting out of the ground and the palm of the hand opened. It was as if the deceased had the briefest moment to reach up to heaven and beg for mercy prior to his passing, "That is rigor mortis—Allah rest his soul." Amira began to weep, and they both remained silent once again.

From time to time, Omar's truck brought them episodes of panic. The line of vehicles was reaching the back-up location that Omar had anticipated. The cars were moving, but it was stop and go traffic for miles. They worried about a breakdown in the middle of all the traffic. Just as it seemed the truck was going to collapse, never to recover, its engine would mysteriously spring back to life. There was still gas left in the truck, but the engine needed water soon.

At one point they knew they couldn't wait any longer and had to stop and let the overheated engine cool down. Smoke was everywhere, but fortunately there was no fire. Once again, they were spared, as they had some of their leftover water which they gave to the thirsty, tired, battered, unsightly, yet faithful old vehicle.

While they waited, Omar parked the truck directly underneath a magnificent old oak tree so they would all have shade from the burning August sun, which had then reached the pinnacle of the afternoon sky. From the back of the truck, Nazar, still in a daze, and Yousif, who remained serene and untroubled, gazed upwards at the mighty tree branches and rich green leaves which filtered the summer sun in beams of sparkling light.

Nazar heard the cheerful sounds of various birds. Then his eyes caught the bright white feathers of the Skylark's belly. *Is it possible*, he thought, *that he has followed us all the way from our farmhouse?*

As the afternoon wore on, the miles to the checkpoint got shorter and shorter. The truck held steady. Omar clutched his prayer beads and Amira said her rosary. The two passengers who were stretched out in the back of the truck slept on and off, somehow able to cope with the August heat and the fumes of the road.

At last, there were only a few vehicles in front of them at the checkpoint. It was almost their turn, so Amira and Omar started to get nervous. The Kurdish soldiers were carrying their rifles, of course, and wore their helmets. They were in full uniform, proudly displaying their many badges and pins which reflected the sunlight. One soldier in particular was very tall. With his stern facial expression and barking voice, he sent out frightening signals to every person he questioned.

Amira told Omar with some apprehension that she would not be able to understand the Kurdish language, which was to be expected, because her routine spoken language in Karemlesh was always Sureth. Omar mentioned to Amira that they were likely going to have a major problem as the Peshmerga would probably only be speaking to them in Kurdish, and that they normally do not know any other languages. He said he knew some Kurdish, as he had lived briefly in one of the territories where the Kurds were in charge. But how much he could remember or how well he could communicate in that language was yet to be proven.

Listening to their rantings back and forth in Kurdish, it sounded to Omar that the Peshmerga were very worried that some of the migrants could be terrorists. They were methodically inspecting the cars and trucks for explosives and various kinds of IEDs. Men, women, and children were searched underneath their clothing to make sure they were not hiding any weapons which they could be carrying with them into the city to cause even more terror and pain.

Some of the refugees were forced by the soldiers to get out of their vehicles, with their guns pointed right at them to reinforce the message. Then, strangely, the travellers did not get back into their vehicles after the search of their bodies was completed. It seemed to Omar like their vehicles were being confiscated by the Kurds, as he observed the soldiers commanding them to take the belongings they could carry, and then go on their way. Omar and Amira heard these frustrated migrants arguing with the soldiers, saying in

Sureth, "This is my car, you can't take it. We own it. We paid for it. We will need it for when we get to Erbil. Give me my keys back! This is not right. We are not terrorists. We are Yazidis. We are a peaceful people. We are not violent." But the soldiers pushed them with the backs of their rifles and forced them to continue the rest of their journey on foot—of course, in the heat of the blistering August sun.

"Now it is our turn, Amira. Take out your rosary again. Start praying some Hail Marys. We don't want to lose this truck, not with our two passengers in the back."

The tall Peshmerga soldier approached the truck with a mean face and an impatient tone of voice. He was wearing sunglasses, so you could not see his eyes. As expected, he spoke to them in Kurdish. He told them he didn't know a word of Sureth. He asked them where they were going.

Omar replied in a very broken and primitive Kurdish, sensing what he was asking, "We are going to the Holy Family clinic in Erbil. We have two ill passengers in the back." They let Omar step out of the truck and point to Nazar and Yousif, resting in the pickup truck surrounded by luggage and satchels. Yousif was awake and smiled at Omar, as if to signal to him not to worry. Omar repeated to the soldier, speaking slowly to help him understand, "These two guys are very sick. We are going to get them medical care as soon as possible."

The tall soldier then spoke in Kurdish in a disgruntled tone to another guard standing nearby, figuring neither Amira or Omar would understand what they were saying, "I know this ploy. They probably have the explosives hidden on that kid, and maybe even on the old man. They think we are stupid." He then went over to Nazar and Yousif and started to vigorously search their pants and shirts. Then he looked at the pile of stuff in the back of the truck and started to unzip satchels and open up suitcases. He almost seemed disappointed that he didn't find anything dangerous, not even a kitchen knife. Nazar's eyes opened during the search, but he was still in a daze. Then the soldier looked inside the front of the vehicle and brusquely commanded Amira to get out. Amira and Omar were searched everywhere on their bodies, with no respect for their dignity or privacy.

Amira had a clever idea, as she had no access to words in Kurdish that she could use to win their trust. She pointed to the truck, showing the tall soldier in gestures that they needed it to bring the two other passengers to the clinic. He stared sternly and suspiciously at her. Then she drew in the sand, right in front of the soldier's army boots, the primitive outline of a fish.

The soldier looked at the fish and thought she wanted to bribe him with a *samak*—perhaps even a *samak mazgoof* or another tasty fish dish. He looked inside the vehicle and saw there was no cooler—and no fish! He walked over to the other soldier and started talking to him, asking him to come and look at the sketch in the sand. The other soldier, shorter and slightly more relaxed and less intimidating, laughed and said out loud in Kurdish, "Christians! I see she is a Christian."

Then the shorter soldier looked at Amira and asked her in Arabic, "I know some Arabic. You speak Arabic?" Amira nodded.

"Are you trying to tell us that you are a Christian? Is that it?"

Amira said yes, of course, replying to him in Arabic. So, speaking in Kurdish, he explained to the taller soldier that the fish was a Christian symbol, and that the message she was trying to send is that she is a peaceful person, a follower of Jesus.

The taller soldier replied back angrily to all of them in his earthy Kurdish slang, "That's what they all say. They pretend to be Christians. Yes, we have let in thousands and thousands of people who say they are Christians—they are entering Erbil this very day. We don't know who is lying and who is telling the truth. We will only find out after a terrorist bomb has gone off and there is bloodshed in the marketplace. And then we will have to clean up the blood and guts and body parts which have splattered all over the place."

Amira gazed at the tall soldier with her hazel eyes. The indescribable serenity which emanated from her face softened his frown. Amira reached into her pocket, took out her rosary beads, and put them into the soldier's free hand, the one which was not holding his rifle.

"Do you have children?" she asked the tall soldier in Arabic, "You know, little ones?" She gestured with her hands to show him she was talking about his children.

He looked at her, but he did not understand what she was asking. So, she asked the other soldier in Arabic if he could be the interpreter, "Would you please ask him if he is a father and has children?"

Understanding at last what she was asking, the tall soldier nodded.

Then, once again, at Amira's request, the other soldier conveyed a message to him in Kurdish, "You can use those beads when you pray for your children."

The tall soldier looked down at the beads and gently rubbed them with his long, calloused fingers. He paused and said nothing for just a few seconds. It seemed like an eternity. He seemed to be pondering Amira's words. Perhaps he was wondering what his life would be like without war, checkpoints and guns, without the constant fear of deception from terrorists. What would his life be like without having to be always hiding behind his icy mask of suspicion? What would his life be like if he could be home with his children and waste just a little time with them—hugging them and laughing with them…Or perhaps he was thinking about one of his children who was tragically killed in this relentless war. Amira and Omar would never know.

Omar thought he saw the smallest tear drop down past the soldier's sunglasses onto his cheek. The other shorter soldier also noticed it, and was amazed by the change, winking at Amira. Then the tall soldier looked away, as if to hide his emotions. He waved his gun, signalling for both of them to get back into the truck, and he sent them on their way.

He Carried You Until You Reached This Place

Only a few days ago, before the exodus from the Nineveh plains had begun, Erbil was functioning as a normal city with cars, office buildings, stores, people walking about at the market and on the sidewalks in their business attire. Here in this bustling city, only a few days ago, there was no immediate fear of the mortars or bullets. There was no shattered glass, no crumbling walls, no fires, no explosions, no Abrams tanks, no extremists shouting Allahu Akbar, no smoking tires, no overturned cars and trucks, no fear or panic in the air. It was a city where people went about their daily tasks while caring for the needs of their families. Erbil was peaceful; it was a place where Christians and non-Christians interacted routinely in cooperation and harmony.

Within a few days, everything was different. Yes, the people who could get to work still continued their tasks, but the streets were now crowded with the thousands of refugees who had flooded into the city from the villages to the west.

Among them, were, of course, Nazar and Yousif in the back of Omar's faithful pickup truck, and Omar and Amira, looking through the windshield at the dire spectacle before their eyes. The streets were clogged with the traffic caused by all the vehicles that had entered the city from the checkpoint. As they passed by the town squares and the parks, small camping tents were everywhere, tents which likely were brought in by the refugees who sensed they might not have a place to stay when they arrived, and they were right. There were lines of people in front of the cathedral and the other churches, new arrivals hoping to get some food and water. There were a few hastily established UN aid stations and groupings of disorganised volunteers scattered in various locations, attempting to attend to the sick and injured. Wherever there were abandoned or unfinished structures in the city, the refugees put down their satchels and blankets and rested there to give themselves temporary shelter.

All of a sudden, in only a few days, the crisis of over five hundred thousand abandoned lives was thrust upon the residents of Erbil. Where could they find enough food, medical care, and shelter for all these people, with so little advance preparation and so little warning? When these basic needs could be taken care of, where would they find work to feed their families? When would they be able to return to their villages? Once again, elderly people and families with small children were lying by the roadsides of the city, hoping someone would come to their aid and bring them food and direct them to shelters. It was heart breaking for Amira and Omar to witness this suffering, but they kept focused on their immediate responsibilities.

With Amira's assistance in navigating, Omar drove directly to the Holy Family clinic in the centre of Ankawa, the historic Christian enclave in the city. They were delayed at many points due to the mayhem of the streets, but at least they were all still alive, and the truck engine was still running on a thimble full of gas. They looked at the crowd of people outside the clinic. They were all trying to enter the building and get emergency medical care, but only a few could be let in at a time. Omar acted quickly to get Nazar inside. There was one young thin attendant with a moustache, who was nervously screening people at the front entrance. Omar ran up the steps and grabbed him by the arm, directing him to his truck. He showed the attendant Nazar and Yousif lying there in the back, and gestured that he would need help picking them up and carrying them in. The attendant folded his arms and insisted there were no beds left inside, that the people in the front of the line had priority, and they should take them elsewhere. Suddenly, Amira stepped out of the truck and said firmly, "My sister is Sister Caterina. She is in charge here. Please bring us to her. It is urgent." So, the attendant nodded, quickly found two helpers to bring in Yousif, this time on a real stretcher, while Omar carried Nazar over his shoulders.

When they entered the lobby, it was chaos, but Amira recognised that at least it was friendly chaos. There were not enough chairs in the emergency area for people to sit on, so many people were standing, their faces dirty, their children crying, and everywhere that the clinic could find a spot, cots and beds were positioned—in every hallway, and even outside the bathrooms. There were a few larger rooms that held 12 or more beds of people of all different ages with differing medical ailments. Many were in pain from war injuries, which made the sound of moaning in the clinic almost unbearable at times.

A burly staff assistant working at the clinic, visibly harried, went to find Sister Caterina, yelling out her name above the noisy chaos, stepping inside different rooms, and running down the various corridors looking for her. Zara, the beloved sister of Amira, and known there only as the mother superior, calmly arrived at the crowded front lobby. As soon as she walked into the room, the desperate refugees grabbed at her sleeve to try to get her attention. She was courteous to all of them, but she walked straight ahead across the room, where she noticed her sister and a stranger with a turban huddled in the corner.

She was dressed in the white medical habit that the nuns wear. A small cross was pinned on her lapel. Sister Caterina looked remarkably similar to Amira, with her height, the hazel eyes, the dark olive skin, and her kind expression. Like her younger sister, there was a beauty in her face which would challenge any artist to capture in a portrait. Maybe such an artist would take the easy way out and put a halo on her head. She had no halo that you could see. For the sensitive observer, there was an inner beauty radiating from her soul, bringing peace and healing to whomever she touched. It was a beauty that would never fade with age.

As a medical worker, Sister Caterina had to be very professional at that moment. She knew every second mattered. Overwhelmed by the surprise visit, she gave Amira a big hug, kissed her father, and without saying a word, looked at her sister and let her know how impressed she was that Amira had succeeded in getting Yousif, Nazar and herself through the war zone into safety.

She asked one of the doctors to take Yousif to have x-rays done on his leg as well as a full examination. Amira went along with her father, leaving Nazar with Zara. Omar said goodbye, promised to remember them all in his prayers, then quickly left the clinic to locate his wife and family.

Sister Caterina did not know Nazar. Amira had briefly explained to her what had happened, how Nazar had courageously guided them the entire way on their journey to Erbil. Zara took charge of him, situating him on the very last empty bed in the big room, the one next to the window.

He is dehydrated, no doubt, thought Zara. *He probably was giving Amira and our father all the water and didn't drink enough for himself. And this wound—I see it is starting to become infected. I have to bring down the fever. I need to get him an IV. It all has to happen right away.*

Every other nurse or doctor was occupied with their patients. There was no one available who Sister Caterina could ask to put in the IV or treat the wound, so she decided to stay with Nazar and attend to everything with as much care and attention as her strength allowed.

He will be OK, she thought, *the next 24 hours will be difficult for him, but once the antibiotic takes effect and the IV gets him properly hydrated, hopefully the fever will come down and the wound will gradually heal. It will take time, but it will heal.*

She looked at Nazar's young handsome face with compassion and admiration. He wasn't talking. She was relieved that he was resting peacefully.

She reflected to herself, *It is quite amazing what this young man was able to do, given his injury and his age. He has such stamina, such determination. He doesn't know it, but he saved our father's life. He saved Amira's life.*

She spoke to him, not knowing if he heard her voice, "Nazar, you are a hero. You are a very brave young man." Then she wiped the sweat off his forehead with a cloth, gave him a kiss, and went off to attend to other patients.

When Zara was talking to him, Nazar was immersed in a very deep sleep and was dreaming. But he was listening…to another voice.

He saw the face of the statue of the Virgin emerging from a starry sky. The face came alive, changing from the white marble of the statue to the radiant face of a beautiful young woman with brown eyes and a warm smile. She was gently talking to the young man and gazing at him with admiration. Mary had arms and hands once again. She touched his forehead, his bruised cheek, and his shoulder—imparting peace and consolation to him.

"Nazar, my beloved, I asked you to be my hands so I could give away my love, and you have done so. Did you know that it was my Son who was carrying you on His shoulders all the time while you were carrying Yousif? Your hands carried heavy water for Amira and Yousif to make the long journey possible, and now they are safe. Your hands gathered the eggs from the barn and fed them at table. You see how I have given away my love through your hands. Do you understand, Nazar? Your hands became my hands. My beloved Nazar."

The room was echoing with loud sounds of babies crying, adults moaning, mothers chattering. The vision of Mary vanished. Nazar was sound asleep and appeared to hear nothing.

Late afternoon turned into early evening, with the sounds of crickets and the birds' evensong.

Late evening turned into the darkness of night. At last, it was completely quiet in the room. The nurses had left the patients to get some sleep. All the lights were turned out. The windows in the room were open and the curtains fluttered in the night breeze.

Only a little while before daybreak, Nazar's fever surfaced again and brought with it the same frightening, relentless nightmares of the exodus from his village.

His ears were filled with the mortar and RPG explosions, the sound of bullets flying everywhere, children crying, mothers wailing, walls collapsing. Panic and fear were in the air, mixed with the putrid smell of burning rubber.

His eyes saw the crowds which were rushing down the narrow streets of the village, desperately pushing against each other to quickly escape. They were pushing against him as he entered the town in the opposite direction.

He saw Amar pounding his fist on the counter in his darkened shop and wailing.

And then he saw his brother Samir and his Uncle Basim, sternly ordering him to take the motorbike and get away, "Get out of here, Nazar, move quickly."

Nazar sped like the wind on his motorbike, then he turned around. He heard two deafening explosions. There was an enormous plume of billowing black smoke and a huge red fire rapidly expanding in front of him. The roof of the farmhouse was ablaze.

Nazar cried out, "Samir, Basim!" But there was no answer. He shook his fists at the skies and cried out in agony.

He was on his bike, speeding towards the village. Next, he was running and out of breath. Then, he was wandering through the empty, lonely streets of Karemlesh searching for his father, knocking on doors, asking everywhere. The streets were endless. He made his way through the labyrinth of the old village, then into the newer part of town. Baba was not there.

In this feverish dream, he was trying to figure out what to do next, when he felt a sudden sting in his arm. He was hit by something sharp. He touched his arm and felt the bleeding. After that, a mortar exploded right in front of where he was standing. Then, all the fierce memories and the merciless images faded into a dense fog.

Nazar's heart was beating faster and faster during the nightmare. He felt the pain in his shoulder as if a knife had jabbed him again. Although one arm had the IV in it and was set up so he could not move it at all during sleep, he started to raise his other arm in the air and began waving it back and forth with a fist, as if he were fighting an unseen enemy.

He was very agitated, still trapped in the terrifying nightmare.

"Baba, Baba, where are you?" he was whispering in the dream, but no sounds came out of his mouth, "Baba come back to me! Baba come back! Come back!"

All was dark. No one in the room seemed to know what torment he was going through or how to rescue him.

He kept waving his arm into the air, with his fist tightly clenched.

And then Nazar's fist pounded in mid-air into someone's hand.

It was a big rough hand, and very warm.

It was the hand of a man.

"Nazar, Nazar, my son, my son, I found you…" the voice of the man whispered.

The spell of the nightmare was suddenly broken.

Still half-asleep, Nazar sensed that someone was sitting on the side of his bed.

Then he felt another big rough hand touch his forehead, "Nazar, Nazar—thank God I found you."

Nazar could not see who it was. He gradually began to awake from his feverish daze. The man wound his fingers around Nazar's fist, which slowly opened up and became relaxed—like a flower opening into the sunlight.

Then he recognised the voice. He knew by the voice who it was.

"Baba, is it you? Baba—you were looking for me—and you found me." Nazar began to cry. His tears poured down from his face like the abundant spring rains of Karemlesh, soaking his pillow.

"Shhhh!" whispered his father, "We don't want to waken the other patients. I am here now. You are not alone any longer—I love you, Nazar."

Then the father bent down and hugged him. He rubbed his fingers in the boy's hair and kissed him.

"I have found you, Nazar."

And his father drenched Nazar's pillow with his own tears.

Nazar held him tight and would not let him go. He kept repeating, "Baba, you are here. Baba, you found me. Baba, you did not abandon me."

Then, holding his father's hand, but suddenly silent and unable to utter a word, the boy gently fell back onto his bed, as if he were lying on a raft sailing down a peaceful stream.

A quiet joy flooded his heart, a feeling of unspeakable wonder at all that had just happened.

It was now dawn in Erbil.

The darkness of night was scattered by streaks of pink in the early morning sky.

Outside the window of the room where Nazar, his father, and the other patients were resting, high in a eucalyptus tree, the Skylark began to sing.

AFTERWORD
by Stephen M. Rasche

In his compelling story, author Paul T. Mascia has transported us to the disturbing historical realities of Iraq in 2014. His characters are caught in a catastrophic and violent web spun by terrorists determined to take over their ancestral Nineveh Plains homeland. These characters have done nothing wrong. They have simply gone about their daily lives in their villages in peace. Through no fault of their own, nor as a result of any personal choices they have made, immense challenges, trials, and sufferings have been suddenly thrust upon them. These innocent civilians—Christians along with Muslims—were the "collateral damage" of war.

While Omar and Amira were traveling on the road through the Nineveh Plains, Omar mentioned to Amira that he estimated about 500,000 people, both Christians and predominately non-Christians, were escaping to the city of Erbil. It was the summer of 2014, so, at the time of this book's publication, we have reached the ten-year anniversary of ISIS capturing the region, with the pivotal city of Mosul falling in June of that year.

Omar was far short with his estimate. The number turned out to be well over one million refugees, one of the largest concentrations of displaced peoples in recent global history, nearly all of whom were converging in the very small geographical area of Erbil and its environs. Although a small international aid presence remained from the prior decade of war, much of this was already well involved in winding down. In the rapid escalation of the ISIS conflict, the overwhelming burden of caring for the masses of distressed peoples thus fell on an unprepared Iraq.

For the more than 200,000 Christians, the majority of them fell to the care of the Church in Erbil under the leadership of Archbishop Bashar Warda. Erbil's Christian district of Ankawa became the primary centre for emergency housing and medical care, just as the story describes. During the days depicted in the story, nearly all clergy and women religious, as well as lay people served meals and volunteered for days on end, trying their best to alleviate the suffering of the displaced masses.

With the abrupt ending of *Nazar's Journey*, the author has left us wondering what happened to Nazar, Amira, and Yousif once they reached the safety of Erbil. By leaving their predicament unresolved, I believe Mascia wants us to feel some of the profound uncertainty and dread the threesome experienced about their future. He is right to do so—this dread lingers still. We do know that many refugees never returned to their Nineveh villages, fleeing instead to the already overpopulated refugee camps in neighbouring countries, and then hoping eventually to emigrate elsewhere to start a new life.

Many families did attempt to go back to their villages after the Islamic State was driven out from Nineveh. Taking back this territory turned out to be a military ordeal lasting for more than two years, so they had to wait until their villages were safe before returning. Those who attempted to return sought to rebuild and furnish their homes, but many who tried to move back found themselves discouraged and threatened by the presence of armed militias, some backed by Iran, who were roaming throughout the Nineveh Plains. Many abandoned their homes once again and gave up on the dream of rebuilding their lives in Iraq. Others tried their best to re-settle in their Nineveh villages, but the lack of jobs and the slow process of rebuilding infrastructure deterred them from staying permanently.

When I arrived at the devastated town of Karemlesh two years after the events of this story together with then Fr. Thabet and his Deacon, the Iraqi Army Colonel in charge of the town at first would not let us in. The town had not yet been cleared for mines and booby-traps and he declared it unsafe for us to go in. But Fr Thabet persevered and ultimately the three of us were allowed to enter, together with one Christian militia soldier as our guard. We were then able to inspect the interior of the Mar Addai Church and witness the desecration first-hand. The statue of Mary had been decapitated, and the hands cut off, just as the author recounts. The headless statue had been placed before the main altar as an intentional act of desecration and an ISIS signature of terrorising the "infidel".

As he was crafting his story, Mascia was not aware that the very same statue of Mary from Mar Addai would later be pieced together and partially restored. In 2021, the statue was brought as a centrepiece to the main platform of the Franso Hariri Stadium in Erbil, where Pope Francis celebrated Mass, blessed the revived statue, and prayed with thousands of Iraqis. It was the first-ever papal visit to Iraq and the Mary of Karemlesh statue thus became the symbol of the renewal of Iraq's Christian community. The statue was then returned to Mar Addai where it remains today as a sign of hope, healing and transformation.

As for the Christians of Iraq, among the oldest Christian populations on Earth, their tragic disappearance, particularly since the start of the Iraq War of 2003, remains an ongoing trend to the present day. Iraq, not unlike Syria, Lebanon, and even Iran, is one of several countries of the Middle East with ancient and highly threatened Christian communities and cultures. We have not only witnessed the tragedy of thousands of innocent peoples of various ethnic and religious backgrounds violently forced out of their Nineveh homeland, but we continue to witness the additional tragedy of seeing these cultures, with all their richness, being steadily eradicated from the Middle East.

When Operation Desert Storm began, for example, the Christian population of Iraq was over 1.3 million. Today it is less than 250,000, which is 20 percent of what it was twenty years ago. Still, today there are signs of hope, such as the new Catholic University in Erbil and the new Catholic Maryamana hospital, both of which serve the Muslim as well as the

Christian populations. Unfortunately, jobs remain scarce and structural persecution against religious minorities remains deeply entrenched. For the majority of the young Christians of Iraq, the temptation to leave remains strong.

The microcosm of Nineveh in 2014 has many lessons for the global community.

As much as we in the West may try to forget the bleak details of the history of Iraq and its many wars, we must never forget what transpired there ten years ago. Persecution, whether referring to the persecution of Christians or those from other faiths, is not a popular topic of contemporary conversation. This pivotal word, intrinsic to the Beatitudes, is often avoided in current discourse among intellectuals, politicians, and even religious figures.

But persecution and genocide are not myths. If individuals are facing serious economic injustice, or the threat of derision, or violence, or even death because of their religious beliefs, that is what persecution looks like. It is a real evil. Too many countries which enshrine religious freedom in their constitutions remain centres of severe inequality and intolerance in this world. Rather than detaching ourselves from this uncomfortable reality, which could be out of sight and thousands of miles away, we can always make the choice to find ways to connect with and help these distressed peoples through works of charity, and, at the very least, through prayer.

By creating the characters of Nazar, Amira, Yousif, and Omar in a simple story, Mascia has given these suffering peoples a face. The author is inviting us to get personally involved in their plight, to feel their pain, and to take action to alleviate it. A final important lesson of *Nazar's Journey* is that genuine religious conversion cannot take place in an environment of fear or violence. As I reflect on Nazar's search for his father, which is such a prominent theme of the story, one is reminded that the search for the mercy, beauty, and transcendence of God, is always a search for an encounter with divine love. Thus, if one seeks to promote authentic conversion, it cannot be done without also respecting the freedom and dignity of the individual. Conversion occurs in an environment of peace, dialogue, openness, intellectual inquiry, and, above all, mercy and charity.

If we as individuals can begin to take these lessons to heart and implement them even in small ways in our world, then the messages such as those of *Nazar's Journey* may begin to take root. In this all too barren world, we can pray for it.

Stephen M. Rasche is author of *The Disappearing People: the Tragic Fate of Christians in the Middle East*. He serves as Vice Chancellor of the Catholic University in Erbil, Iraq, and as Faculty Fellow at the Franciscan University of Steubenville.

Pronunciation Guide

For Nine Key Words in *Nazar's Journey*

Note: The principal accent of each word is in capital letters.

Qaraqosh-	KA-rah-kosh (kosh sounds like the osh in osh-kosh)
Karemlesh-	Ka-RAHM-lesh (lesh rhymes with mesh)
Nazar-	Naz (sounds like oz)-ARE (slightly rolled r at the end)
Mosul-	MOW-sool (sool rhymes with tool)
Samir-	Sam (like am)-EER
Basim-	BAH-seem
Aram-	Ah-RAHM
Ghadir-	Gha-DEER
Erbil-	ARE-beel (rhymes with real)